# A. Michele Henderson

Ardena Henderson Publishing

AMH

ISBN: 978-0692785607

# Disclaimer

The storyline of this series is a work of fiction and does not depict the lives of actual persons. Real life locations and pop culture icons are used for context and relatability. The author reserves the right to reference herself as a writing signature.

amichelehenderson.com

# Table of Contents

# Acknowledgements

First and foremost, I give all honor and glory to my heavenly Father. Thanking Him alone for my life and the sweet counsel of His precious Spirit. To my husband James for your love and support, I continue to count it an honor to be your wife. As we approach our 7$^{th}$ wedding anniversary I am grateful that you chose me, to do life with you. To our son Joshua whose brilliance and intellect is exceeding abundant, I love you forever and ever! To my mother Denise for all that you do, I love you. To my Mom and Dad in love, I appreciate all that you do, thank you. To my cousin Phryne for being my cheerleader, I love you! To the rest of my family I thank you all for your love and support. To my mentors, pastors and church family I love you! Where my girls at? To my besties and sister friends who make this journey so rich and rewarding I love and thank you all. I'm eternally grateful for the support of strong and godly women. To my readers who are as vested as I am to my work, words cannot express how much I appreciate you. Your emails, reposts and inboxes keep me going. Whether you purchased this novel, received it as a gift or borrowed it, I pray that you enjoy it!

# Chapter 1: Desperate Times

**A**va stood in the bathroom stall fighting back tears. She respected Calvin's decency to tell her face to face but she had no idea he invited her to dinner, to break up with her. Once she gathered her composure, she opened the stall door, washed her hands and exited the restroom. Wh en she returned to the table to get her coat, the hostess informed her that Calvin had already left and that she was responsible for the bill. As her emotions got the best of her, Ava handed the hostess her Amex card with tears flooding down her face. Humiliated and hurt while other diners looked on, she signed the store copy with quivering hands. $173.00 for food and beverages, $34.60 for a tip, and another lesson learned. While walking to her car in the cold December air, her tears burned her cheeks before settling into the corners of her mouth. It had almost been six months since she relocated from Denver to Washington, D.C. yet she felt just as empty as the day she arrived in mid-June.

Ava pulled up to the security gate of her apartment building not knowing how she'd driven home. She cried so hard and for so long that she had no recollection of ever starting her ignition. Once she parked her white on white BMW 550i in its assigned space, she cried some more. It wasn't only that she was dumped for the third time in less than a year, it was everything she'd been through. An hour had passed before she got out of the car, entered her high-rise and rode the elevator to the 9<sup>th</sup> floor. Once inside, Ava dimmed her lights and put Mary J. Blige's *My Life* album on repeat. After stepping out of the shower Ava began her nighttime skincare ritual. She loved to pamper herself and always received compliments on her pretty brown skin. She lit 3 Kavaldon candles in her favorite scent *Eden* and poured herself a glass of Truvée Red Blend wine. She found a slice of strawberry cheesecake in the refrigerator and decided to lie on her chaise and wind down. It was almost 3am and Ava was still awake singing with Mary, "If you looked in my life and seen what I've seen." She glanced over at her diary and decided to read some of her entries from the previous months. She began to weep as she read. In all three instances of being dumped, it was shortly after she had sex with each man and shared personal stories about her childhood. Ava realized that she'd given them too much of herself, too soon. She made herself a promise to slow down in the future. "Why was love so elusive?" she thought. She knew she was a beautiful woman inside and out. She kept her hair and nails done, she ate well, exercised regularly and at 5'7" was the perfect size 8. She was tight enough to appeal to men who liked thin women and thick enough to appeal to men who didn't. She knew how to cook, clean and sew. She graduated at the top of her class and as a Pharmacist, Alivia Simone Bright earns a six figure income. She looked at pictures of herself from infancy to the present and realized she hadn't ever been happy. After an exhausting evening of reminiscing and toiling in her mind, Ava drifted off to sleep.

The following afternoon Ava woke up with a splitting headache. She walked to the kitchen to grab a bottle of Essentia water. Thankfully she had the remainder of the week to get the pep back in her step. Like many Pharmacists, Ava worked 7 days on and 7 days off. It usually took her a full day to recuperate from a week of 12 hour shifts but she liked the freedom it gave her during off weeks. As she picked up the phone to confirm her supper date with her best friend Shannon, she heard the stutter tone on her phone and decided to check her messages. The one and only message was from her mother Carol, telling Ava about a huge deal she'd just closed for a big client and that hopefully they'd get to see each other next year; because work would keep her in Japan for the next few months. Numb to her mother's words, Ava knew not to depend on her promises since being a child. Though Carol's aspirations afforded Ava the best schools and exotic presents they withheld what was most important, her presence.

Ava was raised by her nanny Guadalupe, in the Cherry Creek area of Denver since the age of 2 weeks. It was then that Carol paid her housekeeper to watch Ava for a few months, while she accepted a temporary assignment in Amsterdam. Over the years, Carol had become a force in the public relations field and was now the first minority and female CEO of a global marketing firm. Carol's work ethic separated her from the impoverished childhood she left behind in Denver's *Five Points* neighborhood and was the driving force to make sure she'd never have to return. Guadalupe had come to America at 15 years old from Honduras and Carol was her first and only employer. What she lacked in communication and experience, she made up for in love. For the first eight years of Ava's life, Carol would make sure she returned for milestones and holidays but shortly after, came home less and less. After graduating from Pharmacy school Ava decided to start a new life in the nation's capital and Guadalupe stayed behind with her husband and children. Ava could always count on Lupe and was grateful for their relationship.

Shannon smiled as Ava approached their table at STK. When Ava greeted her and sat down, Shannon flashed her new 7 carat diamond ring. When Ava stood back up to hug her, the two women squealed as they embraced. While eating appetizers and sipping cocktails, Shannon told Ava all about Bill's "proposal." After listening to her friend and pledging her support, Ava became the bearer of bad news and told her about Calvin. Shannon told Ava it was time to get with the program and now was the best time to do so. Shannon Keller, an O.R. Nurse was now "engaged" to Dr. William Bradford, a surgeon, who she works with at the hospital. The catch; Bill is a married man with 4 children. Shannon knew Ava's heartbreak was the lure she needed to enter the lifestyle of a mistress. Since they'd met, Shannon sat quietly in wait for the opportunity to convince Ava to indulge. Ava pondered Shannon's proposal before hesitantly agreeing to meet "the perfect guy."

Across town, Lawson merged onto I-495 heading back into Maryland. He grew nauseous by the second as he wondered how to pay for his newest acquisition. Kat had convinced him to purchase a brand new Mercedes S-Class Maybach from Lovehall Mercedes Benz. The two of them were drowning in debt yet she pressured him always to look the part. Lawson Taylor, an architect had been dating Katrina Morgan a hairstylist for eight years. During which time they purchased a $700,000 home in Rockville, a Lexus LS 460, Cadillac Escalade, his and her Ducati bikes, his and her jet skis, a condominium in Miami, three 10ft by 12ft Ultrabeds, diamonds, furs, designer clothes and a 40 foot yacht. Though Katrina has a salon and Lawson has a successful firm, their monthly debts had exceeded their combined take home income of $18,000 per month. With 2 mortgages, utilities, yacht payments, 3 car notes, commercial payments for his firm and her salon, credit card bills and a student loan, Lawson and Katrina had eaten through their cushion and were 10 months in the red.

When Lawson arrived at home, it was nine o'clock on a Tuesday night but the house was full of people: eating, drinking and watching the game. Annoyed by Kat's blatant disregard for a quiet evening alone, Lawson entered their home. As if his day couldn't get worse, Kat's mother Angie was eating Lawson's cowboy cut ribeye and truffle and bacon potato from Charlie Palmer's Steakhouse! "I know you're not eating my game food," said Lawson in an "I wish you would" tone. "I can eat whatever I want to eat in *my* daughter's house," mocked Angie. Lawson had reached his breaking point and swiped the plate across the kitchen island and it came crashing to the floor. Just then, Kat entered the kitchen and asked what had happened. Angie told her daughter that Lawson was being a baby over the food she was eating and an argument ensued between the couple. Angie made it her business to fuel the fire and cause more chaos. Lawson walked away and told all of Kat's company to get out. Kat apologized to her guests and assured them they could come back the following night once she brought her house back to order. As her friends left, Angie told Lawson she wasn't going anywhere so he threw her handbag and coat onto the lawn and when she ran out to get them, he slammed the door behind her. Angie banged on the door for Kat to open it but Lawson told Kat that he would take the car back if she did. Kat loved her mother but not more than her appearance and yelled through the door that she would call her tomorrow.

For what seemed like the millionth time, Lawson told Kat they were in debt to their eyeballs. As if working an 80 hour week wasn't enough Kat told him to take on more clients. Lawson told Kat he was tired and would like to downsize their lifestyle to reduce his stress level and improve his quality of life. Lawson had been diagnosed with high blood pressure a year prior and was recently found to have stomach ulcers. Kat wasn't impressed by his new diagnosis and told him to pray about it. "Pray about it?" Lawson mocked. "Yes," Kat replied. "Pray that God heals me of high blood pressure and ulcers that I received from walking away from Him to serve mammon, in order to pacify my live-in girlfriend whom I fornicate with?," said Lawson. "Ninja bye, that extra stuff doesn't matter you grew up in church and your momma is still there, you'll be alright," Kat said in a dismissing tone. "God doesn't have grandchildren Katrina and that's not how it works," offered Lawson. "Whatever," Kat replied.

Again Lawson told her they were going to downsize their lifestyle because he was tired and needed to improve his quality of life. He said they would sell the condo, the yacht and one of the cars and move to a smaller home in order to pay off their debts. Kat argued that she didn't have any debts because none of those things were in her name. Just then Lawson realized that though he and Kat both paid for them they were in his name alone. She threatened to leave him holding the bag if he downsized their lifestyle. Lawson was fuming and realized he had no way to hold her responsible for her portion of their debt. As he glanced at her it was as if the scales fell from his eyes; in that very moment he realized that Kat didn't love him. Immediately he grew ashamed of what he allowed his life to become. His mother Rita didn't approve of Kat from the beginning and had always told

Lawson not to trust her. His father Bernard didn't care for her either and over the last few years he'd drifted away from his parents, his siblings and the Lord. Lawson told Kat it was over between them and since she wasn't responsible for their debt, she had to get out of his house and leave all of his cars. Katrina flipped out. She cussed at Lawson and threatened his life. She then called her brothers and mother who came to get her and her stuff while Lawson sat on the staircase in tumult. Lawson was rarely reminded of where Kat had come from but tonight he remembered she was just a hood-rat looking for a "come up." Her brothers and mother took pictures of themselves in various rooms and posted them to social media. At one point Kat's youngest brother climbed into Lawson's Jacuzzi in his underwear and poured liquor on himself while Angie snapped photos of him. It was 4am the next morning before the fiasco was over and Lawson was able to shut the door behind the Morgan clan.

The following afternoon Lawson called his creditors to find out how much debt he had. After a few hours the grand total came in at $1,643,317.81. With a take home income of $12,000.00 monthly, Lawson began to panic. His choices had led him down a dark road. He decided to visit his paternal grandmother Hattie who lived in Silver Spring.

When Lawson knocked on Hattie's door she was so excited to see him. She had been the only relative he never isolated himself from. Hattie didn't like Katrina but she knew the power of prayer. After eating two bowls of Hattie's homemade chicken soup, Lawson told his grandmother everything. Her heart broke seeing her grandson in so much pain. Instead of consoling him she used it as an opportunity to teach. Hattie was known as a wise woman from way back. She reminded her grandson that sin always takes you further than you're willing to go and to pay more than you wanted to pay. After a few hours Lawson left encouraged and decided to stop at the supermarket on his way home. During checkout his debit card and 4 credit cards were declined. Just then he realized that Katrina had struck again. Before he could tell the cashier that he'd put everything back the gentleman behind him paid for his food. Grateful and humbled at the same time Lawson thanked him and walked away. Before going to his car he stopped at the ATM inside the grocery store to check his balance, -$1,273.04. Lawson fought back tears because he knew Kat had access to all of his cards and accounts. As he placed his groceries in the back of his brand new car, the gentleman who bought his food approached him.

Lawson grew ashamed by the second for having a car the price of someone's house yet unable to pay for his groceries. The man seemed to be in his late 30s, casually dressed with a confident demeanor and a look of concern. "My brother I can't help but sense that you're in some sort of trouble," the man said. "It's that obvious huh?" replied Lawson with a sigh. "My live in girlfriend of 8 years and I broke up last night because I needed to scale back our lifestyle. I've been working 80 plus hours a week and dealing with stress related health issues," explained Lawson. "We're in debt to the tune of $1.6 million dollars but because everything major is in my name she isn't liable to help me pay for it," said Lawson as his eyes welled with tears. "Now it appears that she's cleaned out the bank account and maxed out all the cards". "Wow," the gentleman said. "That's a tall order but nothing is impossible with God, brother" "Can I invite you to a men's group tomorrow night?" said the gentleman. "Sure," Lawson said. "What's your name?" asked the gentleman. "Lawson Taylor," said Lawson. "Okay Lawson, I'm Ryan Hairston, here's my card if you need anything and the address is on the front." The two man shook hands firmly and Ryan got into his car and drove away. When Lawson looked at the card it read: Dr. Ryan Hairston, Senior Pastor of God's Love Church. Lawson knew at that very moment that God was calling him back to the fold.

# Chapter 2: Spitting At the Wind

**A**va smirked as Dr. Jaxon Wheeler sat on the edge of her bed putting on his clothes. Being a mistress was a breeze. Since their relationship began, he ordered new furniture for her entire apartment, paid her monthly bills and booked a romantic getaway for February in Jamaica. Thankfully, they worked at different hospitals and she still had her independence. Ava sent Shannon an edible floral arrangement and a bottle of Chanel perfume to thank her. Jaxon kissed Ava on the forehead as he headed home to have dinner with his wife. While listening for her front door to close, Ava didn't look at the caller I.D. before answering the phone. It was her father Deitrick calling from Vail. When she heard her father's voice she covered her body as if he could see her. Sitting straight up in the bed, Ava gathered her composure. After making small talk Deitrick invited his only child for a week of skiing and winter fun during the week of Christmas. Ava sat in silence before agreeing to go. Her father moved the receiver from his ear and looked at it in shock. Year after year Ava declined but he continued to ask. Surprised and excited, Deitrick told Ava he would make her travel arrangements and call her in an hour. As Ava placed the phone beside her she knew it was time to face her fears. She was now 25 years old and had managed to avoid their secret for 16 years. Since the night it happened, Ava barely spent time with her father and he always chose to meet in public places, so it could never be addressed.

Ava was 7 years old when she and her father Deitrick Bright began spending Christmas at his second home in Vail. He knew Carol wasn't into being a mother and Deitrick spending time with Ava, was part of the deal. Like the two previous Christmas vacations, Ava was excited to be with her father acting silly and playing fun games. He would buy her a ton of gifts and give them to her over the course of the holiday week. She loved the security and love she received from her father and saw him as her hero. One night, Ava had a nightmare and went to her father's room to sleep beside him. As she ran down the hall toward the master suite she heard music and strange sounds. With tears streaming down her face she entered her father's room only to behold a sight no 9 year old child is prepared to see. There her father was in bed with her ski instructor Mr. Ben. The two men were startled causing Ben to run and ultimately break his ankle. Deitrick was ashamed, horrified and embarrassed that his baby girl witnessed his secret in action. Ava ran back to her room and locked herself in the bathroom. She cried herself to sleep in the bathtub while clenching her stuffed rabbit.

The following morning, Ava woke up in her bed because Deitrick had unlocked the door and placed her there. That afternoon she was on a plane being sent home to Lupe and never spent the holiday with Deitrick again. Over the years it was never discussed, though she never saw her father the same way. He was no longer her hero who could protect her from the world. Her security turned into insecurity and low self-esteem. By the time she was a teen she'd found out that her birth was an agreement between Carol and Deitrick for their own personal agendas. Carol wanted a child to seem maternal and sincere. Deitrick wanted a child so his grandmother would believe he was straight and release his trust fund. The two college friends agreed to get drunk and make a baby. Unfortunately their secret was uncovered when Ava was on the phone with Carol and she didn't hang up properly but instead added Ava onto a 3 way call with Deitrick. Ava was crushed to learn that she was a pawn in her parent's selfish scheme. Since then, Ava judged her worth by her accomplishments and her ability to attract successful men.

Lawson didn't know what to expect as he entered the doors of God's Love Church. As he stepped into the sanctuary there was Pastor Ryan speaking to a small group of men. When Ryan looked up and saw Lawson he called him by name and introduced him to the other men. After meeting Lucas, Andre, Calvin and Maury, Ryan invited Lawson into his office to talk privately since he arrived so early. Lawson expressed to Ryan how he grew up in the house of the Lord but allowed his relationship with Kat and the pursuit of financial security to draw him away. Ryan listened intently and assured Lawson that his experience was more common than he thought. He understood the pressures of providing and wanting a good life. He told Lawson that his inherent desire to be great is due to being made in the image of greatness. Lawson appreciated Ryan's sincerity and absence of judgement.

That evening Lawson shared his story with the 14 other men in the group. He liked how Ryan provided them with a safe place to land. Each man understood the pressures of being a man and the relentless power of the female form. Before the session was over Lawson rededicated his life to the Lord, joined GLC and acquired an accountability partner named Kyle. In addition to the hope he found, he was meeting Jeremiah Coleman the following morning at the credit union so that Jerri could buy his car. As God would have it Jerri had become a New York Times bestselling author the previous year and was finally getting his royalties. His book on marriage had gained momentum after an endorsement from an Oscar winning actor, when it saved his marriage. Since then Jerri had been featured on a host of talk shows and in magazine articles. He signed with a major publisher and went on to sell eight million copies.

Lawson drove home that evening feeling understood and loved. He called to tell Rita his good news. She wept for her son with a heart full of joy. He had just told her what he'd been going through that same morning and less than 12 hours later God was already working it out. Over the next few months Lawson met people who changed his life for the best. An attorney at GLC told Lawson he had a case against Katrina and wouldn't be solely responsible for their debts. Another member bought the condominium in Miami and Pastor Ryan's father, father-in-law and brother's father-in law bought the yacht. Gavin, Evans and Freddie; the 3 men were a comedy show on wheels so Lawson was pleased to sell them his yacht. Shortly after, the 3 retirees began charting the boat and hosting fishing excursions that became quite lucrative. Lawson was able to sell his house and buy a much smaller home in Bladensburg. After 9 months of surrendering his life to Jesus Christ and winning his case against Katrina, Lawson's debt responsibility was reduced to $316,000.00. He knew it would take time to come out from underneath it but he knew what kind of God he served.

Ava was relieved to see Shannon pull up to the curb at Reagan National Airport. She was having a great time with Deitrick until he announced his engagement and forced her to spend time with him and his lover. Ava exploded on her father because he didn't have the decency to rebuild a relationship with her before adding on extras. He accused her of being a bigot and she accused him of being much worse. Before she could pack her things to leave her father threw her belongings over the balcony and told her to act like he was dead. Ava's heart broke; all she wanted was a little time to repair the distance between the two of them and now they were worse off than before. It took her hours to gather her things and make her way to the airport because he kicked her out on Christmas Eve. She waited 9 hours at Eagle County Regional Airport as a standby before boarding a flight with a layover in Dallas. She was hurt, tired, hungry, frustrated, confused and rejected.

Shannon climbed out of the car as Ava began to cry. The two friends embraced as Shannon tried to console her. Before driving back to Ava's apartment where Shannon planned on staying the night, they picked up food and drinks. While Ava took a long hot bath Shannon put on her favorite "Oh no he didn't" play list. The music was usually used for breakups but the tone of the songs still created a morose atmosphere. The two women ate crab cakes, wild rice and broccoli before consuming 4 bottles of wine and 2 pints of Talenti Gelato. Shannon showed Ava the dress she chose for her to stand as her maid of honor during her and Bill's commitment ceremony. Ava thought nothing about Bill committing to Shannon while being a married man and hoped she and Jaxson would do the same. Shannon was careful to only invite a handful of their closest friends to the "wedding" because if word had gotten back to her religious parents, it would disappoint them deeply. Shannon had been rebelling since she could remember. When she was 15 she ran away to be with a local rapper shortly after discovering an attraction to black guys. After a while she realized the type of guys she was attracting weren't headed anywhere in life. In her late teens and early twenties she dated a few athletes only to find out how opposed some black women are about their sons dating interracially. As she got older her sights became set on affluence but outside of sports and entertainment the number of black men to date decreased drastically. After some bad breakups and disappointments an acquaintance introduced her to her current lifestyle and for the past 3 years she's been Bill's mistress. Not only had she met all 4 of Bill's children but she proudly picks out all of his wife Emily's birthday, holiday and anniversary gifts. From the outside looking in nobody would believe Shannon was willing to be the other woman. She was smart, funny and possessed a heart of gold. She looked like she could be Carrie Underwood's sister and often sang her songs during karaoke. Being the other woman spoke to Shannon's self-worth and esteem. Behind the pretty face and confidant façade lays a girl who never felt good enough. She failed at all her attempts to be the pious child that her parents wanted. Her questions about life were dismissed as ungodly and her natural curiosities were deemed as unholy. Everything she did, felt, questioned and spoke were met with disdain. Whether she had a bad grade or a bad day she was told to do penance and her father would often drive her to church for confession. As a 28 year old woman Shannon couldn't be paid to enter a church nor have anything to do with those who attend. She had found solace in her practice of yoga and considered herself to be spiritual.

The next morning Ava went to her favorite café to pick up some coffee and pastries for her and Shannon. While standing in line she caught a glimpse of the shoes a woman at the front of the line was wearing. With the slightest movement they changed colors like a chameleon. As the woman stepped to the side to wait for her order Ava got a full view of the woman's outfit, bag and shoes. Sister girl was not only gorgeous but on the money; wearing an evergreen peplum pencil suit, purple and green single soled holographic pumps and a green Chanel flap bag with rainbow hardware. The barista yelled out "Ardena" and the woman grabbed her coffee. As she walked toward her seat Ava caught a whiff of her fragrance which she immediately identified as Subtle Orchid 10 by Krigler. Ava smiled to herself because she was reminded that class and sophistication weren't dead.

Ava and Jaxson were living it up! Over the past few weeks they'd spent a romantic weekend in the Poconos, traveled to Las Vegas to see Mariah Carey and had just returned from Beverly Hills from a shopping spree. Ava loved Jaxson and hoped that he'd soon leave his wife. She knew they had a two year old daughter and three year old son but her selfish desires exceeded her morals. Living a lie wasn't ideal but Jaxson had proven to be the love of her life. When Jaxson finished bringing Ava's bags up to her apartment, she inquired about the bags that weren't there including the fur coat, diamond Cartier love bracelets and Hublot Big Bang Tutti Frutti watch. Jaxson told Ava those things were for his wife and Ava immediately became envious. How dare he take her shopping and buy things for his wife, it was bad enough that he bought things for his children in front of her, she thought. Ava told Jaxson she thought those things were for her and Jaxson told her she'd thought wrong. Tears streamed down her face as Jaxson left with no regard for her feelings. That night Ava cried all night knowing that Jaxson was at home with his wife and family. Jealousy rose up within her until she became nauseous. Shannon had warned her that being a mistress could lead to envy, alcoholism, drug abuse, depression and insomnia to name a few. She assumed Shannon was being dramatic but realized it was the truth. She was unable to sleep, consumed 5 bottles of wine and sank deep into the sadness that engulfed her. The next morning Ava couldn't get herself together and continued to cry and drink. The following day she called out of work and Shannon went to her apartment and nursed her back to health. Ava struggled through the week since Jaxson hadn't called nor answered her emails or social media direct messages. She began to wonder if her emotional health was worth a few stolen moments of his time. When he returned her call six days later, she concluded that it was.

It was the evening before her and Jaxon's trip to Jamaica when Ava stood beside Shannon as she and Bill recited their vows. The ceremony was conducted by Bill's friend Sam. With only four others in attendance Shannon and Bill committed their lives to one another. After the ceremony the small group dined at a doctor friend's private residence. Ava invited Jaxson but he declined. His declining lead to an argument between them and Ava wasn't sure if the trip was still an option. Jaxson expressed how ridiculous it was for Shannon and Bill to get "married." Ava told him she thought it was sweet and Jaxson told Ava he had no idea she was so simple. His words cut Ava like a razor. Jaxson cited that side chicks needed to stay in their place and leave marriage to the women who are worthy of it. "Why would any man commit to a woman whose willing to be a secret?" he taunted. Ava cried as she drove to the ceremony rehearsing his words. How could a man who made her feel so good, make her feel so bad time and time again? Ava was devastated because she had been told that white men were nicer than black ones and now she knew regardless of color, a jerk was a jerk.She didn't want to bring Shannon down from her high so Ava pretended that everything was well. After all, Shannon had introduced Ava to the same acquaintance who hooked her up with Bill. The woman discreetly ran a dating service for the women and men in their lifestyle. Ava congratulated the couple and told Shannon she would see her after their "honeymoon." Bill was using a medical conference in Hawaii as the backdrop for their getaway. Before she left, Shannon held Ava tightly and thanked her for always being a true friend and never judging her. She removed a diamond pendant from her neck and put it on Ava. The two friends hugged once more and Ava drove home. Once home, Ava dialed Jaxson but he didn't answer. She waited by the phone in hopes that they would reconcile because they always did. After ten days had passed, Ava was forced to face the fact that they were over when the agency called to advise her to refrain from contacting him. She tried reaching him anyway but Jaxson had blocked her from his cell phone and social media accounts. The walls began to close in on her at the thought of living without him. She'd refused to unpack her luggage hoping he'd knock on her door and whisk her away. Once again Ava knew she'd been dumped and threw herself a 12-day pity party until it was time to return to work.

# Chapter 3: Paying the Price

After a long day on her feet Ava was glad to be home. After a hot shower and a couple glasses of wine she turned on the local news while she ate takeout in her bed. The meteorologist was reporting another cold front when she picked up the remote to change the channel. Just then a breaking news story preempted the weather. As Ava ate her food she wasn't prepared for what she saw. A local surgeon's wife killed him and his mistress! When Ava looked up she saw Shannon's car riddled with bullets. By the end of the evening the news reported that Mrs. Emily Bradford had shot and killed her husband Dr. William Bradford and his mistress Shannon Keller. Ava threw up all over her room. By the next day the police were at her job because Shannon's phone records led them to Ava. She had no choice but to confirm the relationship between Shannon and Bill. Ava asked the police to forward her number to Shannon's parents so they would keep her informed about Shannon's arrangements. She used her spare key to Shannon's apartment and gathered a few mementoes and removed items she knew Shannon wouldn't want her parents to find. Days went by and the Keller's hadn't called. She found their number in the white pages but when she called Shannon's sister told Ava she wasn't welcomed at Shannon's services. She also told Ava that God wasn't pleased with her life and it wouldn't be long before the devil showed up at her door. Ava slammed the phone down and grew afraid. How could this be happening? Everywhere she went Shannon's name was dragged in the mud but Ava loved her friend. For the following 6 months Ava went to work and back home and fell into a deep and dark depression. Her condition began to affect her judgement and she was encouraged by her superiors to seek help. After months of denial Ava decided to go to therapy.

The cold winter gave way to spring. Spring became summer and summer became fall. Ava had emerged from months of therapy with a hopeful outlook. She began spending time with Bethany whom she met at the gym. The two women quickly became friends and would frequent the happy hour scene on the DC waterfront. Bethany grew up in nearby Arlington, Virginia and was an administrator for the federal government. Ava invited Bethany to be a buffer during dinner between her and Carol. After two years of rescheduling, Carol finally kept her promise to visit her daughter.

The ladies dined at Black Wall Hitch in Alexandria while Carol spent the entire meal talking about herself. Carol liked Bethany immediately because she was a career woman. After what seemed like an eternity Carol asked Ava how she was adjusting to a new city. Ava told her mother it was fine but that she was having a hard time finding a good man. Carol told Ava that she hadn't found one because there weren't any. "Sweetheart I know we never had the talk but men are only good for companionship, not lifelong commitments. Please don't be one of those women who make a man their entire life while missing out on making great money and taking care of yourself," said Carol. "Concentrate on building a secure life for yourself because you can't depend on anyone else."

Ava was haunted by her mother's tone while Bethany embraced it and joined Carol in a toast to independence. After a few days Carol left for New York where she'd be living for the next year on her newest assignment. She told Ava they would spend more time together since she was now in the United States.

It was a crisp autumn day when Ava decided to make a stop at her favorite food truck. While standing in line she was lost in her thoughts. Just then the finest man she'd ever seen snapped her back to reality. When she came to herself, she realized he was handing her the $20 bill that had once been in her hand. She thanked him as their eyes met and began to smile while butterflies danced in her belly. "I'm Ava," she said without thinking. "Nice to meet you I'm Lawson," said the Adonis that stood before her. Ava couldn't remember the last time she'd seen a man so fine. At 6 foot 4 and 225 pounds stood the muscular, yet thick man candy that was Lawson Taylor. With a Caesar haircut and well defined eyes, nose and lips Ava was mesmerized. Lawson was the perfect shade of milk chocolate with a smile and dimples that sent her into a tailspin. Lawson thought Ava was equally as gorgeous, as she reminded him of Porsha Williams. The two beautiful people exchanged numbers and Lawson assured Ava, he'd call her tonight.

Ava could barely eat her food while she thought about Lawson. That evening Lawson called Ava at 6pm and they talked on the phone till 2am. The following afternoon they met for lunch. After lunch Lawson took Ava to his favorite cupcake stand owned and operated by two of the cutest little girls: Jordyn and Harlow. They couldn't have been more than 5 and 6 years old but Ava admired how Lawson interacted with them. They had such a good time together that they decided to catch a movie. The day following they met for breakfast. Each encounter forged mutual feelings between them and on Saturday evening Lawson invited Ava to join him the next morning for church. Ava accepted with utter fear. Ava had never been to church. Shannon had told her horror stories about the people in churches. Carol also described church as a place where poor people go to feel better about their laziness. Carol was raised in church and left church behind the day she turned 18. She'd told Ava over the years how her mother would make her and her siblings go without meals just to give money to the pastor. Ava knew she liked Lawson a lot and hoped he wasn't too caught up in religion.

The next morning Ava and Lawson arrived at God's Love Church better known as GLC. Everyone was friendly and warm. Ava was pleasantly surprised. During praise and worship Ava let loose and allowed the music to bring her to a better state of mind. She was amazed how good she felt. Before Lawson's pastor preached his wife Blake made some announcements. Ava was surprised how fashionable Blake was. She thought church women wore big hats and matronly dresses. Not only did Blake have on a beautiful silk dress, she had on Louboutin's and wore makeup. Shannon told Ava that church women didn't wear makeup. When Shannon was 16 she was caught wearing lipstick and her mother told her that makeup was for whores. As penance Mrs. Keller made Shannon bathe in scolding water to clean her soul. Pastor Ryan preached a message that left Ava feeling brand new. Church must've changed since Carol and Shannon had attended. She felt uplifted and better than she had when she walked through the door. During offering time the congregation cheered for the opportunity to give and none of the members looked like their children were missing meals so they could give offerings. Lawson saw the look of amazement on Ava's face and inquired about it. She confessed to him that this was her first time in a church and that she'd heard horror stories. He told her that he grew up in church and witnessed horror stories first hand but that God shouldn't be rejected because of man's errors. He explained to Ava that church was an opportunity to celebrate God with other people who have a relationship with him also. He told her that unity, strength and hope are found in assembling with others of like-minded faith. Lawson was excited to share Christ with Ava and prayed that she would come to know Him for herself. During the altar call Ava didn't go up to receive salvation and it was the only part of the service that she felt uncomfortable. Lawson told her the uneasiness she felt was the result of being disconnected from God. "When you belong to Him, you can stand in His presence without fear and doubt," said Lawson in a loving tone. Ava was petrified and wanted the service to be over.

After service Lawson introduced Ava to a few members and his friend Kyle. Ava was shocked when she saw Calvin and pretended that she never noticed him when he spoke to a man beside her. Minutes later Lawson and Ava were escorted to Pastor Ryan's office. Lawson had told Ryan that he was bringing Ava to service and Ryan agreed to meet her. Upon entering the Pastor's office Ava's anxiety had disappeared. Two young children were sitting on the floor playing with their toys. Just then Lady Blake walked in carrying an arm full of dry cleaned clothes. Lawson introduced Ava to his pastor and lady elect. They were a great looking couple who appeared to be in their mid-thirties. As Lawson and Pastor Ryan made small talk Ava watched Blake care for their children and clean her husband's office behind them. After leaving the room for a few minutes Blake emerged with a hot plate of food for Pastor Ryan complete with silverware and a placemat. She brought him a cold beverage in a glass and dessert before she rounded the children up to head home. Lawson ended their visit so that Pastor Ryan could enjoy his meal before a meeting with his staff.

Back in the car Ava inquired about the Hairston children. Lawson told Ava that there were actually three but the eldest was in his teens. He also pointed out that the little girl and boy were twins. Ava found it interesting that a woman who seemed to have it going on like Blake would wait on her husband hand and foot.

During dinner Ava told Lawson that she'd dated Calvin the previous year. Lawson asked if her math was right because Calvin had been married for 3. Ava assured him that it could've only been last year because she had only lived in DC for 15 months. Lawson used the situation as an opportunity to teach Ava that her dealings with Calvin were an example of man's choice to dishonor God and family. Ava was annoyed because she had been a mistress long before she agreed to be one.

After Lawson dropped Ava off at home he thought about Calvin and Ava. He was thankful that she told him the truth but it made him wonder what it was about Ava that made Calvin comfortable to cheat on his wife with her. Lawson secretly hoped that Ava wasn't promiscuous because he really liked her. That evening Lawson and Ava spoke on the phone until the wee hours of the morning. The following week the two were inseparable spending all their free time with one another.

On Thursday night Lawson attended his men's group and told the brothers that he really liked Ava. Pastor Ryan encouraged Lawson to take it slow. He also reminded Lawson that Ava was not saved and as much as he could influence her to live right she could influence him to live wrong. Kyle agreed and told Lawson that he should take his time and be mindful of what God had delivered him from.

Bethany was excited to see Ava after she had seemingly dropped off the face of the earth since meeting Lawson. She listened intently as Ava raved about the food truck and how they met and how fine he was. She told Bethany that he took her to church for the first time and it was great. Bethany was floored. She hadn't ever met someone who never went to church. Growing up in a Methodist household, Bethany thought every decent human being went to church. She told Ava that she was surprised how far Ava made it in life without God. Ava was amused but was glad that Bethany had a better outlook on church than Carol and Shannon.

Later that evening, Ava mistakenly told Carol how much she liked Lawson and that she went to church. "Be careful sweetheart, I told you not to get caught in the clouds. I'm sure he's a decent man but before you know it you'll be waiting on him like a maid." Immediately Ava thought about Blake and how she brought in her husband's clothes, cleaned his office and brought him food as if she didn't have two small children and a teenager to care for. "They use that bible to convince women to submit to a man and become subservient," Carol mocked. "The reason I work hard like I do is so you can see that women don't need men to take care of us or validate us." Carol added, "Besides those scriptures were written to pacify people who are broke and lazy like your grandmother with the hopes of a good life after death! I want a good life now, I'm not worried about pie in the sky," mocked Carol in a bitter tone. "My mother sat around praying and reading that bible when she should've been working after my father left." Carol's voice began cracking and she was fighting back tears. "I wouldn't serve a god that would have me and my children below the poverty line." In response, Ava told her mother that Lawson owned his own architectural firm, owned his home and came from a good family. Carol told her daughter that Lawson's type more than any prefers docile women. She assumed that Lawson's mother was probably a housewife and warned Ava not to fall in love before she angrily hung up the phone. Carol sat on the bed in her motel room crying like a baby. She remembered how drastically her life had changed after her father left and she'd be a monkey's uncle before letting Ava turn into a church mouse. After their conversation all the hope and excitement Ava had about Lawson was completely extinguished.

Later that evening when Lawson called, Ava was distant. She told Lawson that she wasn't feeling well and ended their conversation. The following day Lawson

surprised Ava at work and brought her favorite lunch.
Believing she was just not feeling well the prior evening,
Lawson continued to be smitten with Ava. During lunch
Ava remembered why she cared for Lawson and chose to
never confide in Carol again. The following weekend
Lawson and Ava double dated with Kyle and his wife
Tonya. Ava knew that they were members of GLC and
looked for signs of subservience in Tonya. The entire
evening Tonya was funny and witty, perhaps Ava was over
reacting to Carol's words. During a trip to the ladies room
Ava asked Tonya what she thought of Blake. Tonya
replied, "I don't," causing Ava to laugh uncontrollably.
Tonya agreed that she saw Blake as a weak woman and if
Blake liked it she loved it. That evening Tonya and Ava
became bound by their low opinion of the pastor's wife.
Ava bravely asked Tonya if she and Kyle remained celibate
until marriage and Tonya looked at her as if she had 3
heads. "Girl bye, ain't nobody gon tell me I can't ride the
horse before I buy it," said Tonya. Ava confided in Tonya
that Lawson was celibate and she was over it. Tonya told
Ava that Lawson would give in under the right
circumstances but she would have to create those
circumstances herself. Ava agreed and the two women
returned to the table. That evening Ava invited Lawson up
to her apartment and he declined. The following night she
asked if he would change the bulb in a recessed light that
she couldn't reach. Lawson changed the bulb and left
immediately after telling Ava that they shouldn't be alone
in her apartment. For three weeks Ava tried to get Lawson

to fall but he resisted. One afternoon Lawson picked up Ava and took her to meet his Grandma Hattie. During the visit Hattie was sweet as always. She served them heaping bowls of her homemade beef stew and homemade seven up cake. Ava liked Hattie and felt special that Lawson thought enough of her to bring her to meet his grandmother. The following week was Thanksgiving and Ava would spend it at Lawson's parent's house in Waldorf.

By the time Lawson arrived at home he had a voicemail from Hattie telling him to call her. When he returned his grandmother's call she told Lawson that though Ava was beautiful and well-mannered, there was something off about her. Lawson admitted to his grandmother that Ava didn't know the Lord. Hattie was disappointed that Lawson seemed to be headed down the same road he'd just come from. Before hanging up Hattie reminded Lawson that Katrina didn't know the Lord either and how she would go to church in the beginning just to appease him. Just then Lawson remembered how Katrina went to church with him and slowly lured him away. That evening when Lawson called Ava he told her they had come to the point in their relationship where expectations had to be discussed. He told Ava he wasn't willing to be with a woman who had no intention of seeking a relationship with the Lord. He told her he was 34 years old and past dating and playing house and that he was looking for a wife. He told Ava he would give her the next few days to decide if she was that woman.

Ava hung up the phone in awe of Lawson. She loved how he took charge of the situation yet gave her the choice to choose. The next few days Ava decided within herself that she would move forward with Lawson but be watchful for the signs that Carol warned her of. The following day Ava called Lawson and told him that she was the woman he was in search of and Lawson was pleased. Excited to have love in her life made Ava hopeful about her future. The next day while she was at work Lawson sent Ava a large box of plum eternity roses from Venus Et Fleur. The preserved roses last an entire year. When Ava opened the card it read:

*By the time these roses die you will be my wife, forever*

*- Lawson.*

Ava hadn't ever felt so loved. Aside from her corsage for prom, a man hadn't ever given her flowers before.

During Sunday service Ava sat next to Tonya and cracked jokes about Blake. Behind her back the two women called Lady Blake "steppin fetchin". Since Lawson was always so focused on service he was clueless to Ava's disrespectful ways. During the altar call she went to the altar and got saved. Lawson fought back tears watching the woman he loved, choose life.

On Thanksgiving Day Lawson brought Ava home to meet his parents Bernard and Rita Taylor along with his two brothers Scott and Bernard and his sister Jamie.

Bernard Jr. was married to Kenya and together they had 8 month old baby Kyleigh. The Taylor's embraced Ava in hopes that Lawson was a better judge of character. When Grandma Hattie arrived she told Rita that something was off about Ava. Rita listened but knew there was a time when her mother-in-law didn't like her either. Lawson announced to everyone that Ava was a new convert but Hattie wasn't convinced. During dinner Ava learned that Rita had a successful career as a CPA debunking Carol's assumption that she was probably a house wife.

Over the next few weeks Lawson and Ava were like peanut butter and jelly. Lawson met Carol through FaceTime and Ava was all in. Carol had to admit that Lawson was fine and if she were a decade younger would've given Ava a run for her money. Reluctantly Ava reached out to Deitrick and he agreed to meet Lawson through Facetime as well. During their conversation Ava went to the bathroom and Lawson wrote on a piece of paper and held it up so that she couldn't overhear.

*Mr. Bright, Do I have your permission to propose to Ava?*

Deitrick agreed hoping Lawson would turn Ava into a better person. Before their fight, Deitrick noticed that Ava had poor life skills. He knew he and Carol didn't raise her properly but maybe Lawson would be a better influence. With Deitrick's blessing Lawson was excited and quickly ripped up the homemade sign. Once Ava returned to the conversation she tried to bring it to an end but not before Deitrick introduced Lawson to his fiancé. Lawson was caught off guard and the look of shock was on his face. Ava immediately pressed the button to end the call. That evening Ava told Lawson about what she had witnessed as a child, her ordeal the previous year in Vail and the pact between her parents. Lawson realized that Ava was good at keeping secrets because he had no idea that Carol didn't raise her and Deitrick was homosexual. He knew that Ava was a great person and hoped he could help make her a more open and trusting woman.

# Chapter 4: Half-Baked

On Christmas Eve while drinking hot chocolate and walking along the National Harbor, Lawson proposed to Ava. She accepted as he presented her with a 2 carat princess cut solitaire. Gone were the days of excess for Lawson but he wanted Ava to have a respectable ring. The two embraced and for the first time since being a child, Ava felt safe in the world.

Just days after Lawson had proposed to Ava he called and made an appointment to meet with Pastor Ryan. It was just a week into the New Year and surprisingly he was able to meet with him the following day.

The next afternoon Lawson was greeted by Blake as she escorted him to the church's meeting room. The room was a serene space with a long conference table and a dozen plush chairs. Lady Blake assured Lawson that Pastor would be with him shortly before encouraging him to help himself to the refreshments on the adjacent table. When Ryan walked in he apologized for being tardy as he and Blake were still entertaining friends from out of town since the holidays. After some small talk about the weather and current basketball season, Lawson informed Ryan that he proposed to Ava. He went on to ask Ryan if he would marry them soon. Ryan expressed his concern that Ava was new to the faith and didn't seem ready for marriage. Lawson told Ryan that he was struggling with celibacy and found it harder to hold onto. After a few moments Ryan agreed to perform the ceremony but made it clear to Lawson that they needed to go through 6 weeks of premarital counseling with a couple he'd assign to them. After premarital class Ryan and Blake always meet with every couple for 2 additional sessions. Lawson agreed and Ryan told him to check his email later that day for the counseling schedule.

When he got into the car, Lawson called Ava to inform her about the meeting. Ava didn't receive the news well. She told Lawson that grown people don't need permission from other people as to whether or not they're ready to get married. Lawson felt the pressure of the situation and called his father Bernard. Bernard told his son that there was nothing wrong with checks and balances but he would support him either way. The following week Ava and Lawson were married by the Justice of the peace. Bethany attended in support of Ava, as Lawson's parents and siblings supported him. Absent were Carol who said she was too busy to attend and Grandma Hattie who told Lawson he has her love but not her support. Ava tried to invite Lupe but her telephone number was no longer in service. The following day Lawson received a call from Ryan at the firm when news of their nuptials had spread on social media. Ryan told Lawson that though he didn't take his advice he still wanted him and Ava to take the classes. Lawson convinced Ava that they needed to take them and she finally agreed to go.

After their honeymoon in Antigua, the Taylor's returned to Maryland to begin class. Over the following six weeks they sat with Kai and Lorena Johnson for 2 hour sessions. Topics included everything from finances to intimacy. Most evenings Ava left with an attitude because she didn't agree with what was taught. Her attitude would lead to arguments between her and Lawson which caused great dissension in their relationship. After the 6 classes Kai informed Ryan that the Taylor's seemed incompatible on the deeper issues but since they were married they'd have to work hard in order to stay married. Ryan was disappointed by Lawson's choice to get married but he could only advise his flock not force them to obey.

Ava was so annoyed that they had to meet with Ryan and Blake. She had already decided that she was going to do what she wanted to do whether or not they agreed. During their drive to the church the Taylor's argued the entire time. By the time they reached the church they were depleted and agitated. When they reached the church conference room it was obvious that they weren't getting along. Blake led the opening prayer before Ryan led the teaching. During the session Pastor expressed to Ava that it was important for her to submit to Lawson and not compete. Ava was livid. Carol was right, they were trying to control her and Lawson was letting them do it. Ryan could sense Ava's immaturity and lack of preparedness for marriage. Lawson knew he had jumped the gun but was really struggling with his desires at the time. Blake offered herself to Ava for mentorship but she declined. During the session, offense consumed Ava and she refused to talk to Lawson or anyone else. The following week Lawson attended the second session alone and during the weeks following attended Sunday service and bible study by himself. Ava told Lawson she wouldn't ever return to church again.Ava grew cold and cruel while the Taylor's began living separate lives. Because Ava's lease wasn't up until June she began staying at her apartment leaving Lawson home alone. In an attempt to repair the breach between them, Lawson reached out to Carol. After an earful of bitterness and assumption Lawson realized that Carol was the source of Ava's skewed outlook on life. Carol accused Lawson of wanting a doormat but messing with the wrong woman's child. She told Lawson that real men don't need organized religion and if he wanted a submissive wife he should've married someone with a G.E.D. Carol was worse than Angie and Lawson refused to go back to the hellish life he left behind over 2 years prior.

Ava became more distant towards Lawson once she found out he called Carol. Carol had convinced her that Lawson wanted Carol to help him control Ava. She began going out to the club and only saw Lawson when she wanted sex. She and Bethany began to party and drink throughout the week and flirt with other men. Ava not only danced seductively with other men but would often sit on their laps. There were even times when Ava went over Bethany's boyfriend's house to cuddle up with one of his friends.

After weeks of being alone Lawson confided in the men at his weekly meeting. He expressed that he was in love with who he thought Ava was but now he realizes she is someone else. The brothers offered their encouragement and prayers but knew this was something that he and Ava had to walk out. During the meeting Ryan remained silent concerning the Taylor's troubles.

After an encouraging talk with Kyle, Lawson tried to get things back on track. He began to surprise Ava with show tickets, flowers and gifts of appreciation. Ava accepted the gifts but remained distant toward her husband. Every attempt Lawson made to please his wife proved to be unfruitful.

On a snowy afternoon in early March, Lawson sat in his office drawing blueprints. Losing track of time he realized it had been hours since the last time he'd eaten. He decided to run to a local café and grab a bite to eat. While he sat at a corner table noshing on his sandwich a woman asked to borrow the pepper from his table. As he looked up to hand it to her their eyes locked. She smiled as she took the pepper back to her seat. He hadn't seen a woman smile at him in a while and turned around to glance at her. When she noticed him staring she made a joke that he should just take a picture. Lawson laughed and walked to her table to begin a conversation. Her name was Evelyn and she was in DC on an 8 week assignment for the government. Lawson was taken by her kindness and great attitude. Not only was she beautiful but her life's work included humanitarian initiatives. They had great intellectual debates and after a week of "running into each other", Lawson and Evelyn met at the café for lunch. Her fiancé was deployed in Afghanistan and they were supposed to get married when he returned the following year. Lawson opened up about his situation and found her to be a source of comfort and support. Evelyn became a listening ear and they began to speak on the phone every night. The two of them grew close and Evelyn began to cook for Lawson and brought him meals to take home.

One evening Evelyn went to Lawson's house to retrieve her pie dish and he invited her inside to watch a movie. The movie began to watch them as they began to kiss. Their kissing became deep and passionate and Lawson started to undress Evelyn. He carried her to his bed and undressed himself. That evening and throughout the night Lawson and Evelyn shared their bodies with one another. The next morning they woke up in each other's arms. He knew he was wrong but Lawson received from Evelyn all the things Ava denied him. It wasn't long before they began to spend their nights together. Each time they were intimate Lawson thought about Ava less and less. Evelyn would stop by the firm to have sex with Lawson, during her lunch break. Lawson began to buy Evelyn expensive gifts and stopped calling Ava all together.

Across town Ava lied in bed on her first day off of the week. She realized she hadn't heard from Lawson and grew suspicious. Had he given up on her? Missing him, she decided to drive to his firm so they could talk. On her way to see her husband she decided stop and get them something to eat. Once back in her car she grew excited to see him. She told Tonya how things were going between them hoping she would take her side. Tonya told Ava only a simple woman would push away a good man and asked her where they did that at. Ava assumed she and Tonya shared the same outlook but was sorely mistaken. Tonya told Ava she didn't roll with women who didn't take care of their husbands. Ava was confused because they always made fun of Blake. Tonya informed Ava that she was just joking and Blake was wise enough to make sure her man was covered when half the city wants Ryan. Ava recognized that she was educated but not informed and hoped she could repair the damage she'd done to her marriage.

As she pulled up to Lawson's office Bethany rang her phone. Ava decided to take the call since she knew Beth was on her lunch break. While talking to Bethany Ava watched as a beautiful woman got out of a range Rover and went inside. Moments later Lawson emerged with the woman and walked around to the driver's side door. Ava looked on as Lawson held the woman in his arms and kissed her. With his hands rubbing her body, Ava could tell that Lawson *knew* her. While Beth was in mid-sentence, Ava hung up the phone. Tears began to well up in her eyes and she began to cry. Moments later the woman drove away and Lawson went back inside. Deciding whether to confront him or just drive away, Ava decided on the former.

Lawson sat at his desk eating the lunch Evelyn bought him when Ava walked inside. Surprised to see her but over the drama Lawson looked up in silence. "I see you've moved on," Ava said sadly. Lawson placed a smirk on his face because he was glad that Ava saw them. "What's up," Lawson inquired." "I came to talk to you about us but I see there is no us," said Ava. "Little girl you started this foolishness I just ended it," Lawson replied. "Does she know you're married?" Ava asked. "As a matter of fact she does," Lawson replied with a smug tone. "What kind of woman deals with a married man?" Ava mocked. "The kind like you," Lawson said with a smile. At that very moment Ava came face to face with herself and his words cut her deeply. She felt ashamed and exposed at the same time. He was referring to Calvin but she had also willingly dated Jaxon. Ava stood in Lawson's office and broke down in tears. Lawson was moved with compassion for his wife and he still loved her. He walked over to her and held her. After a few moments she pushed him away. "I can't believe you're cheating on me," Ava cried. "I didn't want to cheat on you but you pushed me away," Lawson responded. "I don't know if I can forgive you," Ava sobbed. The weight of what he had been doing for the past month hit Lawson like a ton of bricks and he still loved his wife. He apologized to Ava and asked for another chance. In that moment Ava knew she couldn't solely blame Lawson for what had happened and chose to face herself and her choices. Ava asked for a week to process her pain before returning home. Lawson agreed and suggested that they seek professional counseling. Ava knew it was time to put on her big girl panties and become an adult. Lawson knew he would have to put on his big boy undies and end the affair that brought him great pleasure and satisfaction. Together they promised to do the hard work of attempting to rebuild their marriage.

Carol sighed as she rang the melodious doorbell adjacent to the massive French doors. It was a blistering day in Denver and her decades old mink coat had seen better days. When Deitrick answered the door he was shocked by her appearance. It had only been three days since his St. John clad "baby's momma" had asked him through FaceTime for a place to stay. She confided in him that she'd been unemployed for almost two years. Instead of scaling back her lifestyle Carol had exhausted every dime she had, playing the part.

The look on Deitrick's face was telling and made Carol self-conscious of her appearance; however, after living in Baltimore while pretending to be in New York, Carol was tired. She had been using an app on her cell phone that allowed her to appear to call from different countries and states. Her fraudulent behavior went undetected until she could no longer pay her cell phone bill. The day before her cell phone service expired, she Face Timed Detrick from a hotel lobby wearing one of her best suits. Still operating in pride, Carol didn't want him to know how dire her circumstances were. He bought her a plane ticket and wired her enough money to make it to BWI Marshall Airport.

After settling in, Carol confessed to Deitrick that she was let go from her job on suspicion of fraud. She admitted that she had taken bribes but due to currency conversion rates wasn't left with much. Deitrick knew the pain and shame that accompanied living a lie and sought to help Carol find her way. It was Carol who had covered his secret many years ago by pretending to be his woman and giving him a child. He was saddened to hear that Carol had meddled in Ava and Lawson's marriage. She told him the guilt she carried for blasting Lawson when he came to her for help, had been the cause of many restless nights. Deitrick knew a good man when he saw one and Lawson was indeed a good man. He privately made plans to reach out to Lawson for Ava's sake.

Ava approached Lady Blake after spotting her at Whole Foods. She was checking off items on her list when Ava startled her from her thoughts. Surprised to see her, Blake reached out and they embraced. After making small talk Ava apologized to Blake for the way she acted during counseling and asked Blake if she was still willing to be her mentor. Blake accepted her apology and encouraged Ava. She then agreed to mentor her on a trial basis and gave

Ava the time and location of her next mentoring session. Ava was surprised that Blake mentored other women but looked forward to seeing what it was all about.When Blake arrived at home she told Ryan about her run in with Ava. She knew she had her work cut out for her because Ava was as deep as a puddle. Ryan encouraged her by using her current mentees as an example of her effectiveness. After listening to her husband's wisdom, Blake agreed to do her very best.

# Chapter 5: Eating Crow

The following week, Ava arrived at the address Lady Blake had given her. It was an office suite on the lower floor of a business complex. Much to her surprise Lady Blake was the founder of an awards gala and a bona fide business woman. "Where does she find the time," Ava thought. When she entered the suite a woman at the reception desk greeted her. When Ava told the woman her name she instructed Ava to go to the third room on the left. As she entered the room four friendly women greeted her as they sat at a conference table. Each of them introducing themselves Lori, Jewel, Sarai and Micah all of whom Ava recognized from GLC. Ava felt welcomed and warm. After the women made small talk and enjoyed light refreshments they heard Blake's voice coming down the hall. When Blake entered the room she was wearing a full length fur which she casually threw over the chair beside her. Her hair was in a tight bun and her makeup was flawless. She wore a black turtleneck with one fish scaled leather sleeve, an Hermes H belt, olive green riding pants and thigh high black suede boots. As a fragrance addict Ava recognized Blake's perfume as Tom Ford's Santal Blush. Ava almost went into shock when Blake placed a black crocodile Givenchy Antigona bag on the table. Blake greeted them with a warm smile and told them to take out their notebooks or devices. The room was called to order just by her presence and Ava realized she had misread Blake completely. The one hour session wasn't a "ki-ki" with a few girlfriends but an intense learning experience. Using scripture references and a book each woman had been reading, Blake laid out the protocol, practice and presence of a woman of God. At the end of the session Blake opened the floor for a couple questions from each woman. Ava was floored to learn how inadequate she was for womanhood let alone marriage. When it was her turn the spirit of God surrounded her and she was unable to pretend. She admitted her unpreparedness for life, womanhood and marriage. She shared about her upbringing, her parent's agreement and her brokenness. Blake was pleased that Ava didn't waste her time because she could sense Ava's distraction with her clothes when she entered the room. As the women encouraged Ava that she had come to the right place and they'd walk through it all together, Blake wrote down a list of books she wanted Ava to read. The other women invited Ava to join their prayer call on Tuesday mornings at 5am and to a weekly fellowship at a local café to keep each other accountable and encouraged between sessions. Ava exchanged contact information and looked forward to having relationships with godly women on the same journey. Blake told Ava she would mentor her for the long haul if she was ready to submit to the process. She agreed and Blake added Ava Bright to her roster. When Ava inquired as to why she put her last name down as Bright, Blake replied that it was because she wasn't capable of being Ava Taylor until she healed Ava Bright. "This isn't a race to restore your marriage, this is a process to restore yourself," Blake explained. If you don't get yourself straight, you and Lawson don't stand a chance but if you become who God says you are, you and Lawson will have a 100% chance of making it," Blake lovingly said. "You'll know you've had a breakthrough when you realize you wouldn't want to be anyone on the planet but yourself." In that moment Ava understood why Pastor Ryan didn't want to marry them and why it made things worse to undermine their shepherd. Ava knew it was time to humble herself and glean from the very woman who she once mocked and back bit. As she slid into her car she called Lawson to apologize. He accepted and confessed to her that he had just left from making things right with Pastor Ryan. He had spent the previous day making things right with Grandma Hattie and they were both on a humble pie tour. When Ava hung up she was relieved that they were getting the help they so desperately needed. Just then she watched Blake get into a steel grey Mercedes G550 and watched her drive off in admiration; not because of what she had but because of who she was.

Over the next couple of weeks Ava moved in with her husband. The couple bumped heads and argued almost daily but they were committed to making things work. They willingly ate the consequences of their choices and knew that if they kept doing the work they'd have a marriage they could be proud of. Lawson waited patiently for Ava to become a woman before she could fully be his wife. Putting the cart before the horse was a recipe for difficulty and disaster and they both had learned an expensive lesson. When Ava checked her email she had two messages from Lady Blake. The first one was the date, time and subject of their next group session with an attached homework assignment. The second was sent just to her with an outline of the steps she needed to take to find wholeness.

1. Admit and accept the truth concerning your struggles and confess them to the Father. 1 John 1:8-10

2. Educate yourself in the areas where you fall short. (Reference the books I've assigned you to read on self-esteem and integrity) Hosea 4:6

3. Practice what you're learning to replace outdated habits with new ones. James 1:21-25

4. Use the gift of imagination to see yourself victorious in your areas of weakness. Use scriptures to pray them into reality. Hebrews 11:1-3

5. Forgive yourself and others for past wrongs and extend to others the grace you seek from God. Matthew 6:14-15

6. Receive a new mindset as you seek to see life through the lens of Christ. Philippians 2:5 Romans 13:13-14

7. Seek God in prayer for your "why." Only He can tell you your life's purpose. Study Ephesians 1 & Romans 8

8. Become who God says you are by strengthening your prayer life and studying his word! This is a life long journey that every believer is required to travel both corporately and individually.

Talk to you soon, Lady B!

Ava printed the list not knowing where all this would lead but knowing who was leading her. She had so much to do that she drew up a schedule for what to do and when. For the first time she felt a part of something secure and permanent. What she lacked in a natural family she was gaining in a spiritual family. Ava knew she couldn't fix everything all at once and decided to focus on one thing at a time. After a time of prayer Ava felt the Lord leading her to deal with her issues of abandonment that have plagued her since early childhood. After looking through the bible for a scripture to anchor her during the journey she settled on Psalm 27:10 (AMP) ***Although my father and my mother have abandoned me, Yet the Lord will take me up [adopt me as His child***]. Ava confessed the scripture aloud throughout the day and rehearsed it in her mind for encouragement. After looking online and scanning popular books she discovered 5 signs of abandonment that were present in her life:

1. Attaching too soon to others
2. Being controlling

3. Finding fault in others
4. Sabotaging relationships
5. Expecting perfection in others

Ava made a list of practical steps to implement when these five signs reared their heads in her day to day life. Included in those steps were getting to know people before sharing private things about herself, if ever at all. Blake taught her that she had to place a value on herself and over sharing devalues her life experiences. She then resolved to allow the people around her to govern themselves because she was only responsible for her actions and reactions. She then decided to see the good in others and not go out of her way to tear people down. Ava progressed in allowing her relationships to take their natural course and allow well intentioned people to be in her space. Lastly she recognized how hypocritical she was to hold others to a standard she couldn't meet herself. As she practiced new techniques and leaned on the Lord she became a pleasant person to be around. She and Lawson began arguing less and she accepted responsibility for her actions and words. Ava knew by conviction that Bethany wasn't a suitable friend for where she was going. Though she attended her wedding she knew Bethany had no vested interest in seeing her marriage flourish. Never once during her "sorry; not sorry" season, did Bethany ever tell Ava to make things right with Lawson. Ava knew deep down that her friendship with Bethany was too costly to keep. Without much effort of her own she and Bethany stopped communicating and Ava erased her contact information. After a few months she had thriving relationships with the women in her mentoring group especially Jewel and Micah. Ava also became bearable to work with at the hospital.

Lawson sat in his car outside of the firm wanting to do cartwheels. He had just licked the stamp on the envelope of his last debt payment from living with Katrina. He thought of life's possibilities now that his past was behind him. Within a three year span his life had changed so much. He was thankful for the strides Ava was taking to save their marriage and he began to see glimpses of the woman he always believed she was. His friend Darren had recently told him that Kat had a child with some dude in jail. He thought to himself that the man was probably in jail for beating up Kat's mother Angie. That woman had a mouth like a pirate and the brawn of an ox. Lawson laughed out loud as he imagined her fighting a man. He then recanted his assumption when he realized Angie could beat a man. Whatever it was he was thankful that he was no longer attached to Kat or her family and thanked God that she never had his child. Lawson turned the ignition and drove to the post office to put his envelope in the drive up box. On his way home he decided to get Ava some flowers before their double date with his college roommate and his wife, Tyson and Veronica Anthony.The Taylor's sat across from the Anthony's enjoying the sights and sounds at Eddie V's Prime Seafood at Tyson's Corner. Ava enjoyed her salmon with broccolini and truffled mac and cheese. Lawson was a steak man and ate a 22oz ribeye without batting an eye. While the men reminisced about their college days the women laughed at their stories. Ava was thankful she had learned not to overshare. There was a peace that came with being reserved. Lawson leaned in to kiss her and tell her she was beautiful which boosted her esteem. She made a mental note to wear something special for him when they got home. Blake had shared with the group that men needed to be validated just as much as women. Veronica invited Ava to the powder room and the two women excused themselves. Upon exiting the stall Ava stood in front of the mirror and reapplied her M.A.C Taraji P. Henson lipstick. She knew she had a long way to go on the journey to self-love but she was able to look in the mirror without hating who she was. Just then she heard a familiar voice say "Hello Mrs. Taylor," she turned her head to see Lady Blake with a couple of her friends. She said hello and gave Blake a hug. She recognized one of Blake's friends as the lady with the bad outfit from the café. Ava kept on moving and she and Veronica walked toward the table. When Veronica asked her who the women were she offered she didn't know all of them but the one she spoke to was her pastor's wife. Veronica commented that Blake was really fly and so were her friends to which Ava responded "her outside can't hold a candle to her inside." "That's what's up," Veronica said with a smile. When the ladies returned to the table Blake told Ryan that she'd seen Lady Blake. As the evening came to a close Tyson and Lawson made plans to go to a game and the ladies bid each other well. Lawson held Ava close as they stood outside waiting for the valet. After sharing a long kiss with her husband Ava looked to her right and noticed someone staring at her. After a few moments she glanced over and locked eyes with Jaxson as he stood with another woman. Pretending not to care, Ava fought back tears as Lawson walked her to the passenger side before shutting the door. Her stomach tied in knots and she began to break out in a cold sweat. On the ride home she just laid her head back, closed her eyes and held Lawson's hand while they listened to XM channel 066.

The next morning Ava called Blake and told her what happened. Blake told Ava that she was still carrying a soul tie for Jaxson. She gave Ava a prayer strategy and encouraged her to fast in order to be free from it more quickly. She gave Ava some scripture references including Isaiah 58 and explained to her what to do and what not to do. Ava took heed to her mentor's words and on the third day of the fast she felt the Lord rip everything connecting her to Jaxson completely from her spirit. Ava stood in awe of the spirit realm! She was able to recognize how much space Jaxson was taking up within her and God replaced the hole with His love. She was amazed in the days following how much more of a capacity she had to love Lawson. It was as if Jaxson silently stood between them the whole time. When she met with the group she shared her testimony. Blake told Ava she needed to get Pastor Ryan's DVD teaching on sexually transmitted demons. She explained to Ava that there are millions of married couples whose lives and beds are full of people that they've brought into the marriage with them unknowingly. If the average person saw themselves in the invisible realm they'd run to Jesus real quick. Without God there is no remedy for the things we contaminate our bodies, minds and spirits with when we live outside of His will.

During the weekly fellowship with the other mentees, Ava told the ladies how big the space was inside of her that Jaxson possessed. One of the other women told her that she had no idea how much company Jaxson carried and how long he'd been living his godless lifestyle. Ava agreed and was thankful that the Lord had found her. That evening during her prayer time, the Lord told Ava it was time to deal with the second part of her healing, letting go of rejection.

Yet again Ava took the steps to improve herself in the area of rejection. Before making her new list she found a scripture to anchor herself and settled on Acts 4:11 (AMP) ***This Jesus is the stone which was despised and rejected by you, the builders, but which became the chief cornerstone.*** The footnote of the scripture read; *the cornerstone is the supreme foundation stone governing the structure of the entire building. All other stones will be set in reference to this stone.* Ava was blown away! Jesus was rejected and he was the standard for righteousness and the creator of those who rejected Him. "If Jesus could be rejected how much more can we be?" Ava quizzed.

After looking online and scanning popular books she identified 10 ways that the spirit of rejection was operating in her life.

1. Passivity
2. Excessive attention to appearance
3. Deeply critical
4. Feelings of inadequacy and inferiority masked by superiority
5. Comparing self with others
6. Using achievements to cover up lack of self-esteem
7. Hidden addictions
8. Extravagant spending
9. Neglect of priorities
10. Isolation

Ava wanted to cry when she looked at the list. It was more overwhelming than the list for abandonment. Rejection was all too real. It was rejection that caused her to be generous with her body, not place value on herself or set boundaries. Ava cried at the thought of getting down and dirty with her stuff. She had done things in her past that she was ashamed to utter. Just then she heard the still small voice of the Lord saying "give it to me." Ava then remembered she wasn't alone. She didn't have to do it in her own strength. God was right there to love her through the process. For the following 2 hours, Ava laid before the Lord telling Him everything she could think of that she wanted to be free from so that she could one day love herself. Ava knew that she needed to see herself the way God saw her if she was ever going to get out of her pit. Each day she fellowshipped with God and grew stronger and stronger. She began expecting a level of courtesy and a standard for how she wanted to be treated. She stopped writing down what she wore each day to avoid wearing the same outfit in the same month. She stopped picking other people apart especially other women based on appearance. She stopped admiring ungodly women based on their appearance. Ava stopped looking down on people who didn't have degrees or professional titles. She began treating everyone the same across the board and became friendly with people she once looked down upon. One woman in particular, Beverly was a pharmacy technician who worked with her. By starting a conversation and being friendly she found out that Beverly rode public transportation, didn't get her hair or nails done and brought her lunch to work so that she could put all three of her children through college. Ava felt ashamed of herself for thinking less of Beverly for not being fashionable. Over time Ava stopped comparing her house, car, marriage, clothes, husband and lifestyle with the women around her. It was hard in the beginning since she'd done it her entire life but she realized how exhausting it was to compete and compare. With Lawson's help Ava stopped drinking wine because it had become a daily companion. She didn't want anything to hinder her progress and found healthier ways to cope and unwind. Ava began to put more money into her IRA and increased her savings instead of buying things just because she could. Ava had learned her lesson about debt in college when her parents had to bail her out so debt wasn't an issue. Still in all she bought clothes she didn't need to impress people she didn't like. She even took the additional step of having a joint account with Lawson where her full paycheck after savings would go. She had no idea that Lawson made so much money and considered it a benefit of her obedience to God. Together they brought home $22k per month! In addition to her new found freedom Ava learned to ask for help when she needed it. Carol always taught her not to need or trust anyone and Ava found those methods to be unfruitful. She learned in her mentoring group that God intended for people to be in relationships with one another. Isolation was just a sure way for the enemy to attack your mind and lead you away from God. Everyone at some point in life has been hurt by another but life moves on.

...

# Chapter 6: The Vow

It was a beautiful Day in May when Ava cheerfully packed her Louis Vuitton Horizon 55 suitcase and Keepall 55 Bandouliere full of cocktail and sun dresses, stilettos, jeweled sandals and bathing suits. It was a few days before her 28th birthday and she was going with Lawson on a business trip to Los Angeles. She planned to swim and shop while Lawson offered a bid to design a new indoor entertainment complex.

Lawson sat at their breakfast bar enjoying the French toast and turkey bacon that Ava prepared for him. He had no idea his wife cooked so well and was grateful she'd decided to turn over a new leaf. They had been getting along so well since seeking professional and spiritual counseling. As a birthday surprise he was whisking Ava away on a birthday trip of a lifetime. Lawson smiled to himself at the thought of taking his wife to Bora Bora. It was on her life list and after all they'd been through it was his pleasure to make her happy.

After a decent direct flight from BWI Marshall to LAX, Lawson and Ava arrived in sunny California. After collecting their bags, they made their way to the pickup zone to meet their car service. The traffic was horrible and they were grateful when the car pulled up to the Four

Seasons. Once in their suite, the Taylor's decided to eat downstairs at Culina. After taking a shower together which led to making love, the Taylor's arrived 2 hours later than planned since having to re-shower and get dressed. The two held hands on the elevator and basked in the afterglow of their afternoon coitus. The modern Italian restaurant was full of locals and travelers and boasted a laid back atmosphere. Ava and Lawson shared a plate of calamari and each had a salad. As an entrée Ava decided on a lamb shank dish called Gambetto and Lawson decided on a 12oz dry aged rib eye dish called Bistecca. They both drank Pellegrino and Ava didn't miss drinking wine since Lawson wasn't a drinker. During dinner the Taylor's enjoyed great conversation and shared their food with one another. Before returning to their suite Ava enjoyed an affogato and Lawson enjoyed tiramisu. Upon returning to their suite, Lawson decided to order a movie and Ava curled up beside him. During dinner Lawson told Ava they had an appointment the following afternoon; boy would she be surprised!

After a relaxing morning Lawson told Ava to pack up all her things because they weren't there for a work trip but to catch a plane to Tahiti and then a boat to Bora Bora. Ava screamed when she heard the news, she always wanted to go. After a terrible ride through traffic the Taylor's made their way through the security check points and boarded the Air TahitiNui plane on a direct 8 hour and 20 minute flight to Papeete. Ava couldn't contain herself, this was going to be the best birthday ever.

Once arriving to Tahiti the Taylor's gathered their luggage and was taken to the dock where they boarded a chartered ferry to the Four Seasons Bora Bora. It was an extremely detailed trip but Lawson was feeling himself for making his wife happy. Once they arrived at the hotel they were escorted to their beautiful over water bungalow. It was late at night but the Taylor's were thankful to have made the trip. After a luxurious shower Ava and Lawson went to bed. The following morning the love birds woke up to the most amazing sunrise they'd ever seen. Bora Bora indeed was a special place. In full Four Seasons style the couple ordered in bungalow dining and enjoyed a delicious breakfast and the breathtaking views. The relaxing atmosphere and romantic setting were just what their marriage needed. Their counselor had urged them a month prior to make a pact to love each other with reckless abandon for six months. Instantly forgiving and without record of wrongs. They called it the vow and were always to be mindful of it when hard times arose. This vacation was sure to make the vow even stronger.

The next morning was Ava's birthday. After making love during the sunrise with the doors open to the ocean Lawson presented her with a new "engagement ring" asking if she would re-marry him on their first anniversary the following February. Ava sobbed and gladly accepted. They wanted to do things the right way in decency and in order. God had blessed them with His grace to call their marriage out of the valley of dry bones. They had everything they needed to make life and marriage work together. Ava's ring though quite similar was a full carat larger making it a 3 carat princess cut but the new ring had side stones. Lawson told Ava the original ring had to be returned to the jeweler once back at home. His long standing relationship with Marco allowed him to trade in her first ring to offset the price, though not having the ring present during the sale.

Later that evening Lawson arranged a romantic dinner in the surf. Ava was excited to wear her new Victoria Beckham dress though her new Gucci shoes and Valentino bag were not needed. They dined on mixed greens salad, beef tenderloin, Marquisian Spiny Lobster, Feï banana, and lemongrass coconut rice. Everything was delicious. They drank a local punch of exotic fresh fruits and sparkling water. For dessert they both chose a mango and vanilla cheesecake with passionfruit sorbet. Ava's 28th birthday was one for the record books. Just when she thought it couldn't get better a fireworks display was made in her honor. That evening, after a wonderful dinner and dancing under the night sky it happened just like Lady Blake said it would; Ava didn't want to be anyone on the planet but herself.

After a six night stay full of relaxation, love and peace the Taylor's returned to the United States. Once again they spent the night in Los Angeles before returning home to Maryland. The timing of their trip was perfect. Ava learned that it was rare to find flights to Tahiti without weeks in between them. She knew Lawson went to great lengths to make her day special and she appreciated him all the more. Ava was even more grateful that she had four more days off because the jet leg, travel time and stress of traveling had taken its toll. Lawson was off for six more days but that was the upside of working for himself. For the next two days Lawson and Ava laid in bed only getting up to shower and eat. Too tired to go out, make love or get dressed, they slept or watched TV.

Lawson sat in his office at Taylor Made, going over the financial records for the second quarter. He recognized a 300% increase in sales by one of his newest employees, Taylor Vance. His other two employees Richard and Quentin steadily brought in new clients but Taylor's architectural designs produced more commissions than both men combined. In fact he earned Taylor Made four times the commission of his coworkers. Lawson knew excellence when he saw it and decided to present Taylor with an opportunity for advancement. Lawson grabbed his coffee and headed to the lower level of the firm where the three men worked. Upon entering he decided to watch his employees through the glass partitions that separated their offices before making his presence known. Richard, an older gentlemen that was a friend of his father Bernard was practicing his golf swing. Quentin, a college classmate and fellow baseball player for charity was watching a TV show from his desktop. Taylor though only 26 was drawing blueprints. Lawson noted his focus and accuracy. Though Lawson was only 34 he knew he would've been much further in life, if he was as focused in his twenties as Taylor. Lawson fully entered the office so he could be seen. Mr. B gave him a wave as he continued to practice, Quentin saluted him as if they were in the military and Taylor never noticed he was there. Lawson knocked on the glass door and Taylor motioned him to enter. Once inside Lawson expressed to Taylor how great his work had been and offered him the opportunity to become his partner. It must've been music to his ears because Taylor with a huge smile said it would be his pleasure. Lawson outlined the terms of the deal which were a 60/40 split with Lawson owning the majority. He gave Taylor eighteen months to buy into his 40% stake but to Lawson's surprise Taylor was able to pay upfront. They joked about the name of the firm not having to be changed. After the legal documents, trade documents, investment filings and contracts were finalized, Taylor Made was a partnership between Lawson Taylor and Taylor Vance.

Ava sat in her mentorship meeting excited for the chance to share. Lady Blake opened the floor for new news before their session began. Ava graciously listened to others and celebrated their successes. When it was her turn she shared about Bora Bora and her new "engagement." The ladies were super excited and happy for her. She spoke of the moment on the beach when she realized she only wanted her life and nobody else's. Blake beamed from the inside because Ava was finding her way. After a time of prayer, the growing group of women took notes as Lady Blake taught on distractions. In true no nonsense style Blake laid out an indictment against doing things that take you away from your god given purpose. Using practical examples of how problems arise in the lives of others that draw your focus away from what you should be doing. Lady Blake mentioned that Christians can become so sin conscious that we assume that if it isn't sinful it must be right to do. "Just because it isn't sinful to bail irresponsible people out of their mess, doesn't mean you were supposed to touch their mess at all," Blake noted. "If God puts something on your plate He also gives you the grace to do it. We get in a world of mess when we get off course doing what seems right in our own eyes." Lady Blake was kicking butt and taking numbers! Before the session ended each woman chose an area of their life they'd been distracted from dealing with that and they pledged to start or restart. Ava thought to herself as each woman spoke about an ignored area of their life. Just as before when it was Ava's turn she felt the Holy Ghost rise up within her. "I have to be brave enough to work through my issues with my father," Ava said quietly. As soon as the words left her lips Ava knew it would be a long journey. It was July and she hoped she could get past the hurt and ask Deitrick to walk her down the aisle in February. As the other ladies were leaving, Pastor Ryan had come to surprise Lady Blake with flowers and lunch. The two of them noticed the look on Ava's face as she was leaving and asked about her countenance. Ava shared with her Pastor and mentor that she struggled with

Deitrick's lifestyle as a Christian. Ryan shared Exodus 20:12 with her. "The scripture admonishes us to honor our father and mother that our days may be long upon the land, this proves two things," said Pastor Ryan. "First, it doesn't say honor your parents if they are good, nice, straight, saved or wonderful. The only prerequisite for our honor is them being our father and mother," Ryan pointed out. "This isn't to say we can't separate ourselves from abuse or ill treatment but we are not to dishonor them," said Ryan. "Secondly, we see that this honor can cause the Lord to lengthen our days." "Could it be that many who die too soon or before their time have dishonored their parents in some way," (Eccl 7:17) quizzed Ryan. "The same Spirit that drew you to the Father is the same Spirit your father can be drawn by," Ryan encouraged. "Do we agree with his choice, no but we have no right to condemn him." "If you decide to honor him by allowing him to walk you down the aisle, you're presenting him with an opportunity to be in the presence of God," said Ryan in a hopeful tone. "It's our job to love people and God's job to change them," said Ryan with a smile.

Ava was so grateful for her under Shepard. His words gave her so much hope in believing that Deitrick could one day choose to live for God. She gave them a hug and thanked them for their time as she excused herself so they could enjoy their lunch. When Ava arrived at home she spent time in prayer. After getting a bite to eat she sat on the floor of her and Lawson's bedroom preparing to do her work. After reading and searching online she found five areas where the abandonment and rejection she felt from her father impacted her life. She searched the bible for a scripture to anchor herself and settled on 3 John 2 (KJV) ***Beloved, I wish above all things that thou mayest prosper and be in health, even as thy soul prospereth***. She also chose to confess the words Jesus spoke to the woman with the issue of blood after pressing her way through the crowd to be healed, "Daughter thy faith has made you whole." Ava made her list:

1. Inadequate
2. Broken
3. Apathetic
4. Distrusting
5. Needy

Ava decided to look up each feeling in the dictionary to get the full measure of its meaning and search for antonyms.

## Inadequate

Deitrick's absence caused Ava to feel inadequate. Her feelings were marked by a sense of having no purpose and she often questioned why she had been born. No matter how much love Lupe tried to show Ava she never felt like she was enough. In her mind if she had been, both her parents would've made an effort to make her a priority. Ava thought about her life and how full it was. She was a child of God, was married to a man who could stop traffic and now had a support system that most would envy. As she sought the Lord in prayer she found him to be all-sufficient. Everything she lacked could be gained in Christ which led her to experience God's power. Over the next month Ava recognized that she was never inadequate just uninformed. She was now armed with the revelation that she wasn't a mistake and was thankful to be alive.

## Broken

Ava had to admit, for the longest time anger was her middle name. She would lash out at the drop of a dime and fought her way through middle school. As an adult she recognized that anger was just her mask for brokenness. She had been damaged and in some areas not in working order. Her defeated mindset would operate from a posture of sabotage. It was through her brokenness that Ava viewed life and she knew she had to change her mind about many of her beliefs. Selfishness was still a major part of her character though she had made improvements. She saw areas in her life that were irregular and sought to find stability. She wanted to be dependable and strong. On a rare afternoon, she stopped by to see Grandma Hattie and gained the wisdom of a lifetime. The two women ironed out their differences and agreed to build upon the love they shared for Lawson. Grandma Hattie had recognized Ava's wishy washy, in and out personality and knew there was a problem with her foundation. She also gave credit where it was due and told Ava she could see that God was with her. Ava became a woman of her word and only agreed to do things that she was willing to do in excellence and until completion.

## Apathetic

Somewhere along the way Ava became numb. She'd been hurt and disappointed so many times that she stopped caring at all. If she didn't expect anything she couldn't be hurt and that's where she lived. Apathy was a deep pit for Ava to get out of because it meant putting herself in a position of vulnerability. Ava thought about the December meal she would have with her father once a year after the incident. The two of them would sit in an upscale restaurant ignoring the elephant. He would ask her about school, who her friends were and if she had a boyfriend. They would talk on the surface as Ava pretended not to notice that Deitrick's current boyfriend would be at the bar or a nearby table waiting for him to finish his obligatory daddy duty. He would take out his checkbook, write her a check and end the evening. Before she could drive, Lupe would drop her off and pick her up and once she got her license she would drive herself. Her father never came to get her but would always meet her there. It was during those times that Ava learned to stuff her feelings down until they disappeared. After years of merely existing she decided she would allow herself to feel, experience and enjoy life. Not allowing herself to care meant not living at all. Ava wanted to obtain the abundant life Christ came to give her. She decided she had enough power working within her to endure the bumps along the journey. Ava made a list of every bad thing she could remember happening to her. It was much smaller than she thought and less painful than she remembered. She sat in the bathtub and cried on behalf of it all. She heaved and strained and accepted the pain and devastation that came along with it. After she gave it her all and every tear was dry she looked up at the clock and only 4 minutes had passed! Ava couldn't help but to laugh. She thought she was really doing something. As God would have it, her strength was greater than her pain.

### Distrusting

Ava was quite young when she learned not to trust. She knew she couldn't rely on Carol but somehow she expected Deitrick to be different. She remembered all the times she couldn't attend the father daughter dance at school. All her friends would brag about their dresses and gifts their fathers gave them for the dance. Each year Ava pretended that Deitrick had some special work assignment that needed his attention. Seeing her friends with their fathers made Ava especially sad. The confidence and sense of identity each girl had, was enviable. Sure she had her father's last name but she couldn't walk in the same assurance as the girls who knew what family ties meant. Over the years Ava's discernment proved to be off as she trusted those she shouldn't have trusted. Through her brokenness she always attracted those who would misuse her and leave her more broken than before. Though men were her primary abusers both emotionally and verbally she chose to shun women. It seemed they were the ones out to get her, since they were the ones who stole her boyfriends. During her study time, Ava's notes from her mentoring sessions proved to be most helpful. She understood that whether male or female trust had to be earned and built. Once people have displayed consistent patterns of behavior based on mutual interests and respect of personal boundaries, a level of trust could be extended. Ava was amazed how far standards and self-esteem could get you in life. Up until now she had no gauge to measure relationships with. Ava knew that maintaining and accepting healthy standards of behavior were practical steps toward being a trusting person.

## Needy

By summer's end Ava had cried, prayed and practiced what she was learning. The final wound Ava had to face was neediness. From the outside looking in, Ava had it all. Since she was a child she had the best of the best. Nobody that knew her would ever describe her as needy since society measures neediness by external lack. Ava's neediness was emotional. For years she was deprived of love, affirmation, security, and care. All of the things that would make a girl feel safe within the world, she was in need of. There are only so many clothes, shoes, and things a person can have before the absence of love and care expands the God hole. After the incident, Deitrick ceased to be the hero of Ava's life. She lost her sense of security and began leaning on the external for validation and worth. If it wasn't materialism it was boys. When she was older it was status and men. Each thing never satisfying that place that can't be filled outside of family and God. The day Ava was separated from her soul tie to Jaxson she had a point of reference for how big the mind can make another human being. Placing that kind of trust and belief in another person turns them into idols. She recognized the unreasonable expectations she placed on others for years, hoping they could be what she lacked. Ava was blessed to have the unconditional love of a man of God who fought for her. Lawson's love was a true expression of how much God cared for her. She vowed within herself to give love as much as she accepted love and to lean on God when matters were too big for her to carry. By putting situations in proper order she was allowing people to be people and God to be God. Ava had an epiphany when she recognized that her father didn't have the tools to give her what she needed. She blamed him for not teaching her who she was but he didn't know who he was either. Ava grew appreciative as she thought about what she might have been exposed to, had Deitrick been present in her life. Perhaps it was best to feel the pain of his absence than to experience the consequences of his presence. That night Ava laid before the Lord and released her father for not protecting her. She placed him in God's care so she could be free of the anger and hostility, disappointment and pain. It was as if God reached deep inside of her and exchanged His joy for her pain. The words of Marianne Williamson were true; unforgiveness is like drinking poison yourself and waiting for the other person to die.

# Chapter 7: A Clean Slate

It was a sticky August evening when Lawson and Ava decided to see a movie. They drove to Bethesda to the iPic Theaters so they could eat during the show. While standing in line to enter the theater Ava ran into Connie Tate whom she'd met through Shannon. The two women embraced and Ava grew sad thinking about her late best friend. During their conversation Ava asked Connie about Shannon's services saying Shannon's family wouldn't allow her to attend. Connie told Ava the services were quite sad and defended the Keller's choice to exclude people they didn't know from attending. Before walking away she told Ava the name of the cemetery that Shannon was buried in and wished Ava well. Once they found their assigned seats Lawson asked Ava if she knew Shannon was William's mistress. He remembered that news story because it was a national headline. Ava told him she knew. Lawson asked her if she condoned their relationship and fake marriage. Ava told her husband that she did at the time because she simply didn't know any better. Lawson understood and flagged a waitress over to order his food.

That evening on their way home, Ava told Lawson that she had been a mistress just like Shannon. She told him though she didn't know about Calvin, she did know about Jaxson. Lawson listened intently as Ava explained her skewed frame of mind and worldview at that time. She told her husband that his infidelity put her in the other woman's shoes and she realized how reckless she was. Though Lawson was shocked, he dug deep within himself and forgave his wife of her past. Ava felt as though a weight had been lifted off of her chest. She knew that God had forgiven her and she could've kept it to herself but she was thankful she chose to tell it.

It was a rare morning during Ava's off week when Lady Blake called. She asked Ava if she could come to the office and help her do some administrative work since her executive assistant was ill. Ava agreed and made it to the office within an hour. When she arrived, Lady Blake was wearing an oxblood romper and gold jeweled flats. Her hair was in a ponytail with height in the front. She had on no makeup and her skin was flawless. As usual Ava's nose recognized her perfume; Jo Malone's Wood Sage and Sea Salt. Blake explained what she needed and Ava was swift to oblige. Ava was astounded by all the hats Lady Blake wore. After a several intense hours of working, Blake told Ava they needed to stop by her house before getting some lunch. The two women walked to the parking lot and got inside of Blake's G-Wagon. Ava complimented the truck and learned it was a gift from Pastor Ryan. While Blake took a quick phone conference on her headset, Ava took in the moment. Lady Blake's name was embroidered into the headrests and her monogram was on her floor mats. After sitting in afternoon traffic they merged onto a scenic road before pulling up to a gated community. The homes were stunning and the lawns were manicured. After a few turns they pulled up to a beautiful colonial style home with a neutral exterior and flagstone. When the four car garage door opened Ava saw a beautiful anthracite blue Mercedes Maybach. She remember Lawson telling her that he sold his to another church member. Ava could tell it belonged to Blake because she noticed the same monogram floor mats as they passed by. When Blake opened the door Ava was taken back by Lady Blake's sense of style. The sprawling home was beautifully decorated. Warm hues of taupe, grey ivory and gold accented by teal, ivy green and plum. When Ava complimented the décor Lady Blake thanked her and said she had help from her cousin who was an interior designer. The two women removed their shoes and ascended the staircase at the front of the home. Ava saw each of the children's rooms as she followed Blake down the hall. Their eldest son was a Dallas Cowboys fan and his room had the team as his theme. Their younger son's room had a nautical theme and their baby girl's room was a pink and gold princess room with lots of floof and sparkle. As they continued down the hall she saw a home office, loft and a full bathroom. At the end of the lengthy hallway were a set of French doors that led to a massive master suite. Ava was in awe! She followed Lady Blake past the seating area into an L shaped walk in closet that resembled a designer boutique. The commercial style shelves lit up as motion was detected. Beautiful clothes hung on wooden hangers and special items were displayed behind glass doors. One full wall was dedicated to footwear and one to handbags. Ava noted the shoe wall arranged by color and the handbag wall arranged by designer. Lady Blake was definitely a Louis Vuitton and Chanel handbag girl. She had some Celine, Givenchy and Saint Lauren but she mainly stuck with the classics. It was then out of the corner of her eye that she spotted the quintessential handbag lover's dream; A 35cm Orange Hermes Birkin bag. Just when Ava thought she had gone to fashion paradise she spotted a floor to ceiling shelving unit lined with perfume. Everything from classics to exotics were on the shelf. With no mention of her worldly possessions Blake showed Ava the boxes of t-shirts they had come for. Together the two women gathered the shirts into an eco-friendly shopping bag and brought them downstairs. Ava felt like she'd been ripped out of a vivid dream as they put the bags in the truck, grabbed some food at Q'doba and returned to the office. For the remainder of the afternoon Ava prepared gift bags for the women of the church for their upcoming women's conference. She was humbled that Lady Blake trusted her enough to see her home and thankful for their relationship.

Deitrick hung up from his private weekly call with Lawson. He was grateful to hear that he and Ava were doing so well. He was even happier to grant Lawson a second opportunity to marry his baby girl. Though he was disgusted with Carol's behavior he appreciated Lawson for doing something he never did for Ava, putting her first. Deitrick looked through his photos of Ava and realized she never quite looked happy. He grew ashamed when he thought of all the missed opportunities he had to be a father. Even after the incident he should've had the fortitude to take charge of the situation and fostered healing between them. At that moment Deitrick decided that enough was enough. He was going to get help for his secret. He was going to seek therapy for what his grandmother's brother did to him as a child. He was determined to be free!Lawson hung up the phone excited about him and Ava's future. Aside from Deitrick's preferences he was actually a man's man, thought Lawson. He wondered what could cause someone to live such a dichotomous life. Deitrick loved to BBQ all year round, his views were extremely conservative, he loved boxing and he didn't wear pastels. Lawson laughed to himself realizing he was rationalizing a stereotype. Either way he appreciated the relationship they were building and hoped that one day he and Ava would build one too.

Carol nervously walked down the hall of the Sweet Briar retirement home. She had ran into her cousin at Cora Faye's Café and was told that her mother Ruth had been living there. Carol hadn't spoke to her mother in over twenty years and wasn't sure why she had come. When she knocked on the door of her mother's apartment, Carol was shocked when her father Colin answered the door. Colin broke down in tears when he recognized his daughter. Hearing the commotion at the door caused Ruth to see what was going on. She covered her mouth in shock when she saw Colin embracing Carol Ann. Ruth shut the door behind Carol and joined in the reunion. Carol slid to the floor as her parents cried for joy. Once she gathered her composure, they all sat on the couch. Carol sobbed "I'm sorry mama" reminiscent of Sarah Jane in the 1959 classic film, *Imitation of Life*. Ruth rocked her prodigal daughter and assured her it was "alright." After a few hours of catching up, Carol found out that her parents had been back together for 18 years. She was so ashamed of herself for running a never looking back. Life had to humble Carol since she wasn't willing to humble herself. She found out two of her siblings had passed on. Her brother Robbie had died of a stroke twelve years prior and her sister Gail died during Hurricane Katrina. Carol shared with her parents about her mistakes with Ava and told them about Lawson. She was surprised to find out that 5 out of her 7 nieces and nephews held professional degrees. She was so determined to "get out" that she robbed Ava of the opportunity to have a family. Ruth told Carol she needed to show Ava a better version of herself stating that "what you do in moderation, your children will do in excess." Carol was proud to announce that Ava was married to a godly man who got her involved in church. Ruth shouted "Hallelujah" and clapped her hands in praise. She hadn't seen Ava since she was 4 but had been praying for her, her entire life. For the following week Carol visited her parents daily. Once Ruth saw that

Carol could handle it; she "read her rights!" Carol knew she deserved it and appreciated her mother all the more.

It was a crisp autumn day when Ava stood in front of Shannon's grave. She thought about their friendship and wondered how Shannon would've fit into her new life. Shannon had been robbed of the opportunity to know God for who He truly was by those around her who misrepresented Him. Ava wondered if there was a place in heaven for people who were abused by religion. Tears began to fall from her eyes as she thought about the last day she saw her alive. The way Shannon grabbed her and wouldn't let go left an eerie feeling in the pit of Ava's stomach. Did Shannon know that her attempt to grab a morsel of what she thought was love would cost her, her life? Did Shannon know she had reached the point of no return when those bullets flew through her windshield? Ava placed the bouquet of flowers she bought with her in the vase attached to Shannon's headstone and said a prayer. She knew it would be her first and last time coming to see Shannon as she drove away in silence.

Later that evening Ava could barely catch her breath. Getting caught up in a competition with Lawson at the gym, Ava had reached her threshold. She knew Lawson was a track star in high school but he still had it. Trying to keep up with him on the treadmill at 6 miles an hour, Ava had to press the quick stop button five minutes in. She was an elliptical and circuit training kind of girl. Since she lost their bet she had to give Lawson a full body massage; with the body that *he* had, Ava had already won!

The next morning Ava had a brunch date with Micah and Jewel. They'd become so close that Lady Blake called them "JAM". They decided to drive to the DC Waterfront to board the Odyssey brunch cruise. It was a great fall day for sailing. During the cruise the ladies had a ball eating and dancing. The food was delicious and they decided to include the men next time. Jewel was newly married to Grayson and Micah was engaged to Perry. After the cruise the ladies decided to ride to Tyson's Corner for some retail therapy. As usual Ava had to pick up a new fragrance and chose Liberty Island by bond no 9. She decided to pick up a new cologne for Lawson and treat herself to a new pair of Louboutin's. Micah treated herself to a new pair of Choo's and Jewel Bought a new coat. The ladies decided to have an evening snack before each driving home. They also agreed that from now on, they would ride in the same car. Ava stopped by the cleaners when she made it back in town to save Lawson the trip. As she exited with their things, she found herself face to face with Jaxson. As they walked past each other without uttering a word, Ava felt nothing.

It was October and the air began to change. It was time for long sleeves and cute boots. Lori informed the group that Lady Blake's birthday was just days away and so all the mentees decided to surprise her with cheesecake and a group gift. Sarai picked up some balloons and an edible arrangement on behalf of her children. As they heard Blake's voice travel down the hallway they could also hear the small voice of her daughter Rayne. As Blake entered the room, she was taken back by her surprise. She thanked all the women for their thoughtfulness as she greeted them each separately. Always one to slay, she wore a cream pantsuit with wide legs and a fitted blazer. Her hair was down and her makeup minimal. She had on snake print platforms with a matching bag. Ava being the scent hound that she was, immediately recognizing the smell of Chanel Coco Mademoiselle. After sitting Rayne beside her, Blake set up her tablet with headphones so Rayne could watch a movie. Once she was settled the ladies presented Blake with a group card which included a gift certificate for a spa day. In her usual fashion, Blake taught an awesome lesson about forgiveness. Using herself as an example, Lady Blake shared her journey about forgiving her father. There wasn't a dry eye in the house. Thankfully, Rayne's giggles brought joy to the room as her small voice put everything in perspective. After a discussion about goals and their progress since the last meeting, the ladies enjoyed a slice of cheesecake and sparkling cider. Ava and Sarai agreed to be accountability partners since both women weren't in relationship with their fathers. The other three women were blessed to have grown up with and still be close to their dads.

Lawson was dancing to his favorite jam when he noticed an incoming call from Denver across the television screen. When he answered, it was Carol. As he braced for impact a sincere and new Carol had called to apologize. Lawson was floored. For the next hour he and Carol enjoyed a great conversation until Ava came home. When he handed the phone to Ava she quietly sat listening as her mother apologized. She told Ava the truth about her job, living with Deitrick and reconciling with her parents. Ava began to sob. It hadn't been 2 hours since Lady Blake taught on this very topic. She was so in the vein. Carol invited Ava and Lawson to join the entire family in Denver for Thanksgiving. When she checked with Lawson he said it was cool so they agreed to talk soon but see each other next month. Ava turned to Lawson in total disbelief. He told Ava he was waiting for her to cuss him out when he answered the phone but instead he received an apology. Ava told Lawson about class and he agreed that all the signs were confirmation that it was time. After a long hot shower and an epic love making session, Ava promised Lawson she would call Deitrick in the morning.

The following morning after another dose of Lawson's love for courage, Ava Face Timed her father. When Deitrick allowed the call he was pleasantly surprised to see Ava smiling at him. Ava told him she'd been working on herself and how she'd forgiven him for not being there when she felt she needed him most. Tears fell down Deitrick's face as he apologized to his baby for not being in his rightful place. He apologized for the incident and all that happened within her that night. He knew she was afraid and too young to fully comprehend what it all meant. Ava broke down into the ugly cry as her father pledged to do better. He allowed her to say and ask him anything she wanted and he responded in total honesty. Deitrick's willingness to take responsibility as the adult in the situation allowed Ava to rest in her father's words. He promised to take his role seriously and never harm her again. He confided in her that he was working through the abuse he endured as a child. Ava was heartbroken to learn that her father's pain was rooted in a secret. She noticed he wasn't wearing his engagement ring and he made no mention of his fiancé. They agreed to talk once per week and both looked forward to Thanksgiving. As Ava ended the call, she felt clean on the inside as a new wave of healing swept over her soul. Lawson held his wife from behind and told her he was proud. He also confessed that he and Deitrick had been speaking for months. Ava felt secure in having a husband who knew what was best for her. She rested in his arms in awe of what God can do through a willing vessel. Never in a million years did she think she'd spend Thanksgiving with Grandma Ruth and Grandpa Colin. If God could change Carol he could change anyone.

It was October 18<sup>th</sup> and the national holiday known as Lawson's birthday. At Lawson's request, the celebration would take place in Baltimore. Ava, Lawson, Jewel, Grayson, Micah and Perry took the short ride to The Prime Rib steakhouse. The upscale steakhouse was the perfect backdrop for Lawson's 35<sup>th</sup> birthday dinner. The couples enjoyed great conversation over great food. An array of seafood and steak dishes lined the table with an assortment of side dishes. It was a great feeling to have friends who were more like family, thought Lawson. During dessert Micah and Perry presented Lawson with a gift card to Charlie Palmer. The table erupted with laughter. Lawson had recently shared with everyone how Angie was eating his food the night he and Kat called it quits. Jewel and Grayson gave him tickets to the Wizards and Celtics game. Ava told Lawson she would give him his gift later and the table erupted again with laughter. After a great evening with friends the couples prepared to leave. Ava, Lawson, Jewel and Grayson were staying in Baltimore overnight while Micah and Perry were returning to their separate homes since they weren't married. They were just weeks away from their early December nuptials and falling after a year of waiting wasn't an option. The Taylor's and the Babineauxs drove to the Four Seasons in Baltimore's luxury district to check in for the night. After sharing a ride in the elevator to the same floor they agreed to meet for brunch the following morning before driving home. Once in their room Lawson and Ava unpacked before taking a shower together. Before Ava could put on the new lingerie she had purchased for the evening, Lawson carried her to the bed. The two made love all evening and early the following morning. They wore themselves out and were late for brunch and barely made check-out. When they joined Jewel and Grayson at Wit & Wisdom, it was obvious they had a long night. Still, they enjoyed great conversation and good laughs. After brunch they decided to take pictures on the harbor before returning home.

When the Taylor's arrived home, they slept until the late evening. After dinner Ava was finally able to give Lawson his present, a Cartier watch.

Carol and Ruth were walking the aisles of Whole Foods when Carol spotted Lupe. Thinking Lupe would be excited to see her Carol approached her with an excited face singing her name "Luuuuupe." Lupe looked up with a confused look on her face "Do I know you," Lupe asked. "It's me Carol," Carol replied. Lupe couldn't believe her eyes, Carol looked rough. "How you doing?" Lupe replied with an attitude. "Ava has been trying to contact you for months," Carol said matter-of-factly. "Look, I've given you and your daughter my entire life and I want to be free to enjoy what's left," Lupe announced before walking away. Carol immediately grew ashamed. Guadalupe was just a girl when Carol left her with Ava with no regard for either of them. Though Ava would be hurt that Lupe wants to move on, Carol knew she'd understand. On the way back to her parent's place Carol told her mother what happened at the store. Ruth told Carol it was just the beginning because she had given many people her butt to kiss, throughout the years. Carol sighed as she thought about all the bridges she had burnt.

Across town, Deitrick was feeling good. Therapy was coming along quite well and he had a major breakthrough. While singing along to *Uptown Funk* at his favorite bookstore, his and Bernie's eyes met. The two laughed as they were both singing "Don't believe me just watch." After exchanging glances Detrick introduced himself. During a short conversation, they exchanged numbers and agreed to meet for coffee. Both of them wished each other a great day before Bernie checked out and Detrick returned to the shelves.

It was a week before Thanksgiving when the mentees sat in the conference room waiting for Lady Blake to arrive. In true fashion they heard her voice traveling up the hallway before seeing her face. As she turned the corner all the ladies wooed at the sight of her. Just returning from a family photo shoot she was fully made up with bone straight hair and a middle part. Not to disappoint Ava, Blake wore a red Burberry trench coat, a black leather dress with a bow at the neckline, black stiletto leather booties and Tom Ford eyeglasses. The coup de grâce, a Chanel maxi flap in lambskin with silver hardware. Ava had been officially served and she loved every moment! As "LB" hugged her she inhaled the sweet scent of Black Opium Nuit Blanche. Before teaching, Blake asked the ladies how their last assignment went. Ava told everyone about the FaceTime with Deitrick, the reunion between her mother and grandmother and reuniting with all of them the following week, for Thanksgiving. Sarai also had a praise report since going to the prison where her father was incarcerated. The other ladies cheered as some healing took place for their sisters. For the following hour the ladies took notes as Blake taught on the importance of a powerful prayer life. As the meeting ended Blake wished the ladies well as she wouldn't meet with them again until January. The women were sad as if they wouldn't see her on Sundays and Tuesdays but they loved the personal time they shared with her. Lady Blake could sense their mood and told them it would go by quickly and reminded them they had Micah's wedding to look forward to. Not wanting their time together to end all five women decided to have dinner together at Nando's Peri-Peri.

# Chapter 8: Reconciliation

It was the Tuesday before Thanksgiving and Ava and Lawson sat in the first class cabin holding hands on their flight to Denver. The two of them would be staying at Deitrick's house during the trip. The family would be dining at Tara's house, who was Carol's sister's daughter. She had just bought a new home in nearby Polo Club. During the flight Ava expressed her anxiousness to see her grandparents. She hadn't seen Ruth since childhood and never met Grandpa Colin. When they arrived at the baggage claim, Deitrick was already there waiting. Ava gave her father a huge hug and asked him what was different about him. Lawson noticed it too though he couldn't place his finger on it.

During the ride home, the three of them had a great time. Deitrick told Ava that Carol would look different because she no longer could afford the Crayola people to draw her face back on, quoting Chris Rock. Lawson laughed so hard he couldn't breathe. Ava was afraid because of Deitrick's tone. She had never seen her mother look regular and had no point of reference for a broke Carol. When they pulled up to Deitrick's sprawling 6 bedroom home, Lawson was still laughing. "What do you do again?" asked Lawson. "I'm an estate planner,"

Deitrick responded. "You are?" asked Ava. "What did you think I did?" Deitrick inquired. "Nothing," responded Ava. Immediately all three of them erupted in laughter again. When the 3 car garage opened it revealed a shiny black Mercedes Maybach. Ava reached in front of her to run Lawson's back as he pretended to cry. Deitrick asked what was wrong. Lawson told him how he used to have the same car but had to sell it when he couldn't afford to keep it. "I never told you but Lady Blake has one too," Ava stated. "You can have mine," Deitrick said to his son. "For real?" Lawson asked. "Yes, I will have it sent to you once you get home. Consider it my wedding gift to you." Lawson began to cry for real. Ava was shocked that her father was willing to give away such an expensive car. Deitrick hugged Lawson and felt good to be able to give him the car. He wanted a reason to buy the new Bentley truck and now he had one. He decided in his mind he would let his Escalade go and get the Bentley. Before they entered the house Ava asked Deitrick why he had an Escalade, Mercedes and a Civic. Deitrick told Ava he bought the Civic for Carol. Ava knew Carol had truly been humbled. When they entered the house Lawson was still overwhelmed by his father's generosity. When they entered the foyer Deitrick showed them how to arm and disarm the security system. As he was talking Carol came to greet them. Ava was shocked to see her mother. Somehow her courage and audacity came from her former appearance. Standing before her was a meek and lowly Carol. A stunned Lawson was amazed by how ugly

Carol was. She must've undergone plastic surgery each morning to look like her old self. He'd never seen someone look so drastically different without their makeup. Carol had gone from a fox to a stonefish. He realized that Ava looked like Deitrick and silently prayed that she would never take on Carol's features. Carol knew her appearance was a lot for her children to get used to but was tired of being someone else. Deitrick fought back his laughter when he saw the look on Lawson's face. Deitrick showed Ava and Lawson the rest of the house while Carol started on dinner. Once they were in their room Deitrick told Lawson about the look on his face. Lawson told his father that he wasn't prepared for such a drastic difference in Carol's features. Ava told her father she was glad she took after him. Deitrick agreed.

Over a yummy dinner of salmon, brown rice and spinach, Carol told Ava about running into Lupe. Ava agreed that Lupe gave up a lot to take care of her and hoped that one day she would change her mind. That evening the four of them played scrabble and watched Wolverine while eating Carol's homemade pecan pie. The following day they would go see Grandma Ruth and Grandpa Colin before the ladies' appointment at the bridal dress shop.

The next morning Deitrick made French toast and bacon before everyone left for the day. He had a secret movie date with Bernie. Ava and Lawson rode with Carol to her parent's place. Ava had Carol stop by a florist so she could bring a fall bouquet to her Grandma and a fruit basket for her Granddad. Ava was nervous when they approached the door to her grandparent's apartment. When Ruth answered the door and saw Ava she broke down in tears. Her beautiful granddaughter was now a woman with a husband. Colin couldn't believe his eyes, Ava was beautiful. Ruth saw how fine Lawson was and did a double take. For the following hour Ava and Lawson filled Grandma and Grandpa in on their lives. Ruth was grateful to Lawson for bringing Ava to the house of the Lord. Lawson stayed with Colin while the women went to the bridal salon for Ava's fitting.

Once the ladies arrived at the bridal store, the owner Rachel told Ava that Deitrick had already stopped by so they could verify his credit card. Ava tried on four dresses before she found the one. She decided on an Ivory trumpet style gown with sheer panels and crystals. Ruth didn't like that the top half resembled a corset but kept it to herself. Carol cried as she recognized how much of Ava's life she missed out on. Ava chose a spectator with an attached veil instead of a traditional one. While Rachel charged Deitrick's card for the dress and spectator Ava thumbed through a bridesmaid catalog. When she spotted the perfect trumpet style dresses for Jewel and Micah she asked Rachel if the dresses were available in her area. Rachel checked the vendor's system and they were available at a store in Maryland. She wrote down the address to the bridal shop and told Ava to get there as soon as she got back home to make sure they'd arrive on time. Rachel gave Ava her receipt and told her the wedding gown would arrive at her house by the third week of January.

Deitrick was having a wonderful time with Bernie. They had so much in common. He loved how much class and sophistication Bernie had and looked forward to spending more time together. Deitrick told Bernie about Carol staying at his house and how Ava and Lawson were in town. After the movie they grabbed a quick lunch before making plans to go out the following week.

After a great day with her mother and grandmother Ava was excited to meet her cousins the following day. She hoped they would all get along and continue to keep in touch. When they arrived at home, Deitrick had made his famous Seafood Alfredo with salad and crusty bread. He was in the family room, drinking sangria and singing along to Freddie Jackson records. While Lawson and Ava ate dinner, Carol took a shower and changed clothes. After dinner the four of them played spades and watched Denzel Washington films before they all fell asleep on the massive sectional couch.

It was Thanksgiving morning and Lawson and Ava were in the shower making love. Lawson thought it was the only acceptable place to have sex with his wife under her father's roof. Deitrick was in the kitchen with Carol making breakfast humming to himself. Carol pointed out how happy Deitrick had been and asked if he had met someone. He admitted that he did and told Carol to mind her business. Carol knew something was different about Deitrick and admittedly never saw him so happy. When Lawson and Ava made their way to the kitchen, the four of them ate at the breakfast nook. Pumpkin pancakes, sausage, home fries and fluffy scrambled eggs were served. Deitrick and Carol drank mimosas and Lawson and Ava drank sparkling cider. Deitrick felt good having the kids there and secretly hoped they could stay. He hoped the next time they were together as a family; Carol would be out and Bernie would be in.

After a relaxing morning, everyone got dressed so they could make their way to Tara's house. Around 3pm Deitrick, Lawson, Carol and Ava climbed into Deitrick's truck. It was a beautiful day. The air was crisp and the foliage that lined each street were the perfect hues of orange, red, and yellow. When they arrived at Tara's the driveway was quite full so Deitrick parked on the other side of the street so they'd have no problems when it was time to leave. When they rang the doorbell, Tara answered. Carol introduced Ava and Lawson to her niece. Tara was the oldest grandchild and had known Deitrick since being a child. Upon entering the house Ava met her mother's living siblings, her cousins, their spouses and significant others and two of her grandparent's longtime friends. Ava's cousin Danielle was especially smitten with Lawson and thought he'd be better off with her. She flirted with him behind Ava's back to no avail.

Everyone was having a good time and Ava was exchanging contact info with her family. Lawson and Deitrick were hanging out with the men watching football. When it was time to eat everyone gathered in the family room for prayer. Ruth led the prayer and Grandpa Colin sliced the turkey. While everyone was eating the doorbell rang. When Tara returned from the door it was their youngest cousin Bria and her new boyfriend Quantrell. Ruth immediately saw him as trouble and made a mental note to pray him away that evening. After dinner and dessert the family gathered in the basement to watch the movie *This Christmas.* As the evening was winding down Quantrell took out a gun and told everyone to give him their wallets and purses. Not knowing if he was serious some of the family hesitated causing Quantrell to fire a warning shot. Passing around the garbage bag he provided, everyone emptied their pockets and handed over their belongings. Lawson was glad he put his wallet in Deitrick's armrest. Ava privately removed her license and bankcard during the commotion and put her engagement ring in her mouth before handing over her new Louis Vuitton Mélie bag. Deitrick handed over his wallet after also removing his license and cash and Quantrell was none the wiser. Everyone was then ordered to remove their jewelry and place it on the coffee table. Lawson tried to hide his watch but Quantrell was looking directly at him. Ava was heated because she just bought him the watch for his birthday. Ashley sobbed knowing her family would be disappointed in her. Ruth's friend Ms.

Ethel was so afraid, she took off her wig and placed it in the trash bag with her purse. Before leaving Quantrell who had come in a taxi with Ashley demanded the keys to the BMW he saw in the driveway. Carol's nephew Rodney handed over his keys. Deitrick was glad he parked across the street making his truck look like it was at another house. When Quantrell left everyone started yelling at Ashley. Once the police arrived, Rodney activated the recovery system on his car. That evening it didn't take long for the police to locate Quantrell but all the items he'd stolen weren't recovered. The police figured that he must've stashed them somewhere because he hadn't had enough time to sell them. By the time everyone gave their account of what happened and described their stolen items, it was past midnight. Tired and annoyed Deitrick, Ava, Lawson and Carol returned home knowing it could've been worse. Ava and Deitrick cancelled their credit cards before getting ready for bed. That night they decided to purposely sleep on the sectional so they could all be together in one room. Carol's nerves were so bad that she sat up half the night drinking scotch.

The following morning, everyone was still in shock by the robbery. Ava and Lawson decided to stay in while Deitrick went black Friday shopping and Carol drove to her parent's house.

On Saturday Ava and Lawson spent time with Ava's grandparents before returning home to pack for their Sunday morning flight. On their last evening in Denver,

Deitrick fried fish, hush puppies and shrimp. During dinner Ava asked Deitrick to walk her down the aisle as he accepted with tears in his eyes. Carol told Ava they'd be at her wedding with bells on and thanked Lawson once more for sticking it out with Ava.

The following morning, Deitrick drove his children to the airport. He was sad to see them go but looked forward to their wedding. He told them both to call him when they got home and hugged them tightly. As he watched them enter the terminal he fought back tears. As he put his truck in gear to leave, his phone started to vibrate, it was Bernie. Immediately his countenance lifted as he answered the phone.

When the Taylor's landed at BWI Marshall they couldn't happier to be home. As they drove home Lawson told Ava he'd log on to louivuitton.com and order her a new bag, wallet, coin purse and cosmetic case. She was grateful and told Lawson she'd replace his watch. When they arrived at home they called Deitrick to tell him they were home before taking a shower and crawling in bed.

The following Tuesday Ava met Jewel and Micah at the bridal shop to order their dresses. She chose a deep burgundy color called port and brought home the color swatch for Lawson to coordinate the men. When she arrived at home her dress had arrived for Micah's wedding which was only a week and a half away. She and all the ladies were bridesmaids in Micah's massive wedding party. The dresses were floor length with a high neckline and open back in a true holiday red. Ava was excited for Micah because she was a 28 year old virgin. Ava had never known someone as self-confident and comfortable in her own skin as Micah. Just days later, all the women in Micah's life joined together for her bridal shower. Ava was taken back by all the great women Micah knew. Her mom and sisters each gave a speech about the great woman Micah was. A slideshow documented her childhood and her accolades in school. Lori spoke on behalf of the group and presented Micah with a framed picture of the five of them. After a wonderful afternoon of food and fellowship Micah opened her gifts and took pictures with everyone. Ava and Jewel bought her a gift certificate for a couple's spa day. Lady Blake had a previous engagement but sent Micah a beautiful peignoir set.

The following Saturday afternoon, Ava and Lawson walked the aisle in Micah and Perry's wedding. It was the first time they witnessed a Pastor Ryan wedding ceremony. They loved how the vows were biblical and made no mention of sickness or poverty. Ava realized what she cheated herself out of but was thankful for February's do over. The room erupted when Pastor Ryan announced Mr. and Mrs. Perry Jordan. The reception was a blast and the food was beyond great. The Taylor's danced all night and partied with the wedding guests long after the Jordan's left. It was truly a celebration. Micah and Perry would be leaving for their honeymoon in

Australia Monday morning but would have Sunday all to themselves.

It was Christmas Eve and Ava and Lawson were having family dinner at his parent's house. The house was buzzing with people and holiday cheer. It was a Taylor family tradition to host family and friends dating back to Rita and Bernard's 2<sup>nd</sup> year of marriage. Children were running around and everyone was happy. Ava wanted to enjoy herself but had been nauseous for a few days. Lawson noticed that Ava was really struggling and told the family they were heading home since it was beginning to snow. Rita packed up some plates for them to take home including Grandma Hattie's triple chocolate cake. On the way home in Lawson's new Mercedes, he told Ava he thought they should stop by a convenience store to get a pregnancy test. Ava agreed and they stopped at a 24 hour mini-mart. When the Taylor's arrived home Ava took the test. Three minutes later a bright pink line confirmed that Ava was indeed pregnant.

Lawson was excited and Ava was shocked. They agreed to keep it to themselves until the pregnancy was confirmed by Ava's gynecologist. Then, they would tell their parents immediately and everyone else after the first trimester. The following morning Lawson could care less about gifts. He was going to be a father and that was the best gift ever. He secretly hoped for a boy but planned to tell others that he just wanted a healthy baby. After Face Timing with Deitrick and Carol, Ava opened her presents. Lawson gifted her with a new MacBook, a diamond tennis bracelet and waist length fur coat. Ava bought Lawson a cashmere coat, a 2 station drafting table for his home office and 3 bespoke suits.Shortly after the New Year, Ava's doctor confirmed her pregnancy. Though Ava had a November cycle she was actually 10 weeks pregnant. Ava began taking prenatal vitamins once the home test was positive but was surprised to be so far along. They called their parents and grandparents to share the news and Rita was so happy she cried. Ava couldn't help but tell Micah and Jewel who also cried in excitement.

After what seemed like forever, the ladies sat in the conference room waiting for Lady Blake to arrive. Looking through Micah's wedding and honeymoon photos they became emotional all over again. When Blake entered the room they were beyond excited. When she took off her coat to reveal a baby bump they went wild! Ava announced her pregnancy and felt honored to be pregnant at the same time. Blake was floored to find out that Ava and Lawson were victims of a Thanksgiving robbery. Instead of their usual class, Blake told the ladies it was time to make their annual vision boards. With foam boards, glue, scissors and stacks of magazines, each woman would make a visual representation of their top 10 goals of the year. As a point of reference, Blake showed them hers. It included delivering a healthy baby, getting her award ceremony televised and sending 3 students to college. After a couple hours each woman had a clear and defined outline of what they sought to accomplish. Included in their goals were Sarai getting her baked goods in stores, Lori going back to school for her master's, Ava becoming a consulting pharmacist, Micah opening an etiquette school and Jewel writing a book. Before they were finished, Blake surprised them with a mock holiday dinner. Her assistant brought in dinners from a local soul food restaurant. The ladies dined on smothered turkey wings, green beans and mac and cheese. For dessert they had red velvet cupcakes and washed it all down with sorbet punch. After a fun and productive evening, class was adjourned until late February to make time for Ava's wedding and honeymoon.

## Chapter 9: In Right Standing

Carol sauntered into Deitrick's master suite to borrow his electric steamer. When she entered the door to his walk in closet a burst of color caught her eye. There sitting on the floor was a massive imperial saffron and cobalt blue, Louis Vuitton shopping bag. Deitrick wasn't the type to leave his purchases in their bags so she knew it was a gift. Since he was at the dealership buying a new car, Carol decided to take a peek. While sitting on the floor she gently removed the packaging so she'd be able to put it back. After a few minutes she opened the box to reveal a Louis Vuitton Kimono bag, in monogram canvas and bois de rose leather. She stood up and placed it on her arm remembering the days when she would drop thousands during shopping excursions, without batting an eye. She could see herself carrying the bag with a midi length pencil skirt, tweed blazer and silk blouse. As she stood in front of the mirror playing make believe, Carol caught a glimpse of herself and began to cry. Sliding down the wall in melodramatic fashion, she began to sulk and pout. Laying on the closet floor taking stock of her life, she was sure not to crease or scuff the bag. After a short time she regained her composure and sat up straight. Still in all, Carol was hoping Deitrick had purchased the bag for her. They'd been getting along and she really deserved a treat. As she placed the handbag back in its box and slid the decorative ribbon across the center, she realized it was probably for Ava.

It was the week before Ava and Lawson's wedding when they received a surprise FaceTime from Deitrick. He called to tell the couple that he decided to bring someone special with him to the wedding. When Ava asked who the special person was, Deitrick told her it was his new love Bernie. Lawson told Deitrick that he was welcome to bring whoever he wanted and how they looked forward to seeing him. Deitrick gave them a smile and told them he'd see them both at the rehearsal dinner before hanging up. Ava decided to take Pastor Ryan's advice and just love and honor her dad. Lawson agreed and they looked forward to seeing him the following week.

Ava breathed a sigh of relief when she put on her wedding gown and it fit. Since she had lost weight before beginning to gain, she was exactly the same size she was in November. Everything was falling into place and she couldn't have been happier. She slipped out of her gown with Jewel's assistance and prepared to make airport runs to both Reagan International and BWI Marshall Airports. Her grandparents were arriving first and her mother would land a few hours later. Deitrick would arrive the following day and meet them at the rehearsal dinner.

Across town Lawson was grabbing a quick bite to eat before heading to pick up his and Deitrick's tuxedo. His father and brothers had already picked up theirs. A coin toss decided that his brother Bernard Jr. would be his best man and his brother Scott would be his groomsman. A bowling game decided that Jewel would be Ava's Matron of Honor and Micah would be her bridesmaid. Since Micah had recently gotten married she no longer qualified to be Maid of Honor. Lawson and Ava decided not to have a huge wedding party since they were already married and chose to keep it simple.

The following evening the wedding party met for dinner before going to the church. The mood was joyous and light. They'd rented out a room at a local seafood restaurant and were having a great time. While Ava and Lawson stood by the fireplace to have a private moment, Deitrick approached them. After greeting his children he stepped aside to introduce Bernie. "Lawson and Ava I'd like you to meet my bae, Bernadette Powell. Bernie baby, these are my children Lawson and Ava." Ava and Lawson stood in utter disbelief. Bernie looked like Garcelle Beauvais with the class and distinction of Diahann Carroll. Ava admired her cashmere coat, tweed blazer, pencil skirt, silk blouse and sky high pumps. Lawson gave Deitrick the "I see you bruh," look. They each hugged Bernie and thanked her for coming. Carol was talking to Rita when Deitrick approached the table to meet Lawson's family and introduce Bernie. Carol was not only floored but immediately she grew jealous. To add insult to injury Bernie was carrying the handbag that she tried on in Deitrick's closet. Everyone was pleased to meet Deitrick and Bernie and thought nothing of it since they knew nothing about his past. Grandma Ruth leaned over to Carol and told her she was glad to see Deitrick with a woman because she had heard in the streets that he liked men. Carol was annoyed. He had her if he wanted to be with women. Over the course of the evening everyone enjoyed themselves, but Carol was trying to find something wrong with Bernie.Once everyone arrived at GLC Pastor Ryan was also surprised to meet Bernie. Deitrick was definitely a manly man and Ryan repented for expecting something else. Once they had a moment alone, Lawson inquired about Bernie. Deitrick told Lawson that during his therapy sessions he realized he wasn't into men. He instead thought he must've been gay since his uncle had abused him and began to practice his former lifestyle. Lawson was moved with compassion for his dad and was sorry that his young mind accepted abuse as identity. Lawson told Deitrick that Bernie was a baddie and complimented him for choosing so well. They shared a private laugh when Deitrick told Lawson that he understands why men go crazy over the female form. Just then, Carol startled them and bluntly asked Deitrick why he wasn't with her. Deitrick looked Carol straight in the eye and told her after all the years of not knowing who he was, he deserved a woman who was fine. Carol was hurt that Deitrick could be so cruel. She knew she didn't meet society's standard of beauty but she wasn't a dog either. Lawson awkwardly walked away as the two of them continued to have words in the corner. Bernie saw the squabble between Deitrick and Carol from the opposite end of the sanctuary and remained unbothered. She chose to walk with Deitrick through his new season and supported him 100%. It was nobody's business who or what Deitrick use to be and Bernie trusted that Deitrick had closed the door to his past.

The following evening Lawson stood at the altar as Ava glowed and sauntered down the aisle. She was beautiful and Lawson was thankful that they each decided to fight for their marriage. As she walked toward him he realized the vow had really worked. They were so busy loving each other that they never noticed when the 6 months had passed. One year to the day that they traipsed into the courthouse to get married, they did it right. Before their family and close friends, they pledged their lives to God and one another. Deitrick sobbed in gratitude that Lawson hadn't given up on his baby girl. Bernard, Rita and Grandma Hattie were pleased that they'd made it work. Blake was moved with joy to see that her mentee had found her way. Carol was still upset and couldn't enjoy what was truly happening.

During the reception, the guests had a ball. The live band performed covers of their favorite songs and Ava and Lawson danced all night. The guests dined on Italian appetizers, entrees and desserts in addition to the signature mocktail called the "Lava." Guests took photos in the booth wearing silly props and made custom sundaes at the ice cream bar. Grandpa Colin forced Carol to dance and by the end of the evening she began enjoying herself. She looked forward to starting her new job as a bank teller when she returned to Colorado. It was time to walk through her process instead of fighting it. She decided to ask Pastor Ryan if he knew of a good church in her area, and he did. Everyone around her was making giant leaps and a relationship with the Lord was their common denominator.

After a fun-filled evening, Lawson and Ava left their reception to check in to their suite at the Mandarin Oriental in D.C. The following evening they would be leaving for their 2$^{nd}$ honeymoon. They were so grateful that their family and friends came to a weekday wedding just so they could keep their date. The following morning they joined their parents and grandparents for brunch before everyone returned to their respective homes. When Bernie was in the restroom Deitrick told his children he would soon be proposing to Bernie. He said they'd been in sin long enough and she deserved to be his wife not his lover. The Taylors' were excited for him and told him they supported his decision. Everyone said their goodbyes and exchanged contact information while floating around tentative dates for the baby shower.

That evening Lawson and Ava boarded their flight to Las Vegas. So much had come full circle. Not only was Ava married to Mr. Hot Chocolate, but she was returning to Vegas as an honest woman. They enjoyed live shows and great food during their stay. A drunk man gave Ava a few chips to cash in while they walked by the casino floor of the Palazzo. When she went to the cashier, they were worth $5K! When they returned to the Wynn, Ava spent the money on a new bag. She told Lawson that the wealth of the sinner was laid up for the just. Lawson told Ava that a new bag wasn't a just cause and she couldn't stand on that scripture. Instead he offered her the b clause of Psalm 84:11. Just then, they were reminded of how far they'd come. They use to argue and cuss but now they were applying the word of God to their day to day lives.Once the Taylor's arrived back in Maryland they were informed about an ordeal Pastor Ryan and Lady Blake had been through. Not only had their niece been kidnapped and found 3 days later in Chicago, but Lady Blake had to spend the remainder of her pregnancy on bedrest. Pastor Ryan had charged all five of Blake's mentees to begin teaching women's bible study in her stead. Each of the women agreed and Ava began teaching the women in the congregation from her experiences of breaking through. God was so economical that he was using her process to help other women, who wouldn't serve a God like Him.

On a spring morning Ava sat by Lady Blake's bedside watching movies and eating tacos. Both women had pregnancy cravings for cilantro and looked for every excuse to consume it. During their visit Lady Blake shared about their niece Nya's abduction and how she and Pastor Ryan raised her when his cousin battled alcoholism. She then shared about their oldest son from Pastor Ryan's previous relationship and how she cared for their son's younger sister. Ava realized that when people see someone like LB from the outside with her beautiful family, home, cars and designer clothes they have no idea the cost she's paid to be blessed. LB had survived everything from rape to scandalous lawsuits yet she still trusts God at his word. Blake had given Ava priceless pearls that she'd treasure all her days and was honored to be in her presence.

While enjoying their family and friends at a co-ed baby shower in June, Ava sat opening their gifts. The crowd "oohed and ahhed" at the sight of the tiny clothes. The baby had everything she needed. It had only been a month since the Taylor's settled into their new 5 bedroom home in Upper Marlboro, Maryland. Deitrick and Bernie had been in town for two weeks going overboard in the baby's nursery. The baby wasn't yet born but had a ride on Bentley and tufted full size princess bed, beside her crib. Deitrick and Bernie's wedding was scheduled for September and he took pride in being a Pop-Pop. Carol had an apartment and was promoted to head teller. Her process had been painful but each day she grew stronger. She regretted not making wise choices and was hurt that she couldn't do for the baby what Deitrick was able to do but she learned to accept where she was.

Though the baby wasn't due for three weeks, Ava's water broke as she opened the gifts. With the family in hysterics, they began to shuffle around as if they were playing musical chairs. Taking charge of the situation,

Lawson carried his wife to the car and called their doctor. After 2 hours of labor, Eden Alexandria Taylor, entered the world. Named after her mother's favorite scented candle, she became the light of her parent's lives. As the days turned into weeks and the weeks turned into years, Ava and Lawson remained faithful and strong. Together they became parents twice more to sons Drew and Parker and godparents to Grayson and Jewel's daughter Grace and Tyson and Veronica's son Vaughn. After a couple years of faithful membership and service, Pastor Ryan ordained them as deacons and their testimony has saved over 2 dozen marriages.